I0690744

ENSLAVED BY A MAFIA BOSS
2

Brickhouse

DEDICATION

To my husband, Derrick. Thank you so much for your sacrifice. You have my back through whatever and I will always adore you for that. Thank you for not complaining the long nights I'm on this computer chasing a dream that's larger than I ever imagined. You're irreplaceable.

Love You Forever and Then After That!

Your Apple Spice.

Published by Phoenix Publishing House, LLC.
ISBN-13: 978-1-955235-06-8

Published by:
PHOENIX PUBLISHING HOUSE
P.O. Box 154855
Lufkin, TX 75904

BRICKHOUSE

ABOUT THE AUTHOR

Author Brickhouse, born and raised in the hot and charismatic Houston, Texas, has always had a way with words that captivates those who dare to pick up one of her books. She's been writing since the tender age of five. Her imagination has grown even more through life experiences and those she encounters.

Her writing career began when she published her non-fiction testimony under another pen name. That act of obedience catapulted her into multiple genres over the years. Formerly known as Author Shaunessy Blu, she rebranded and relaunched under her current pen name Brickhouse. Same flare, personality, and drama with a more evolved vision for her writing career. She has always been an indie writer, so she learned many hard but rewarding lessons along the way.

She takes pride in creating relatable characters that will have you angry, laughing, crying, or all of the above. There's never a dull moment between the pages of a Brickhouse book! Just ask her Facebook group The Brick House! They get all the deets before the rest of the world. They are constantly wondering when the next book is dropping!

Author Brickhouse writes only what she can feel. So, come on a journey that is guaranteed to have you in your feelings.

Feel free to connect with her via:
Instagram: @author_brickhouse
Facebook: Author Brickhouse

SYNOPSIS

The anticipation continues as Lexington races against time to find his wife and unborn child. He's turning the city upside down and painting it red with his rage. Unbeknownst to him, his father's betrayal and side schemes will bring their empire to its knees. Dasante is oblivious to the fact that his son has fallen in love with Averly Grace.

Averly Grace is losing hope that her husband and father will come to her rescue. A seizes a window of opportunity that leads to a shootout that jeopardizes her and the baby. It seems as though falling in love was the easy part when it comes to solidifying their marriage. Keeping them and their new baby alive is a whole other task within itself. Enslaved by A Mafia Boss Book Two won't disappoint.

CHAPTER ONE

JUANITA ALVAREZ

Twenty-Five Years Ago

"You're not built for this, Alvarez!"

The sudden and forceful tremor sent me sprawling on all fours, "Uggh!"

Williams and I were sparring in the ring. His abrupt blow to my gut knocked the wind out of me.

Despite what he said, I was determined to prove that I deserved to be on the Bloody Five case.

"You're just pissed because you got passed over for that promotion," I returned the favor with a blow to his balls.

"Arrgghh," he instinctively grabbed them with both hands.

"I can handle myself just fine. I have to go. I'm going to be late."

I was chosen to go under cover as the maid for the Saccone family. It was supposed to be for intel, but I felt it would evolve into more.

I had already been living in a small apartment for almost two years just in case the Saccone's tried to look into my past. We expected them too.

I showered and put on some rugged jeans and a black t-shirt. I pulled my hair back into a ponytail and hurried out the door.

I managed to make it to the Saccone mansion on time.

"Glad you could make it," Elenor, the mistress of the house, greeted me.

I was shocked when I studied the case file to find out that Neri Saccone was married to a black woman. She was beautiful, but the Italian's normally stuck with their own like us Latinos.

Elenor was gorgeous with her long sandy brown hair with eyes that matched. She was soft-spoken but what she said held weight.

"Thank you for this opportunity," I shook her hand.

"You can thank my husband. He's waiting for you in his study. Once he's done speaking with you, please meet me in the kitchen. It's down the hall that way," she pointed.

"Okay, I will."

"Neri, Juanita is here to see you."

"Okay, send her in."

She stepped to the side and allowed me to walk into her husband's office.

"Leave us, dear."

"Okay, my love."

He waited for her to leave. Once the door was closed, he proceeded, "We will only have this conversation once. I'm not sure if you're familiar with the Saccone name, but we're an immensely powerful family. With power comes enemies. You will see things and be required to do some things that may be deemed deplorable. Once you've proven yourself, you'll see how beneficial being a part of this family can be.

His cold black hair was neatly tapered. I've never seen green eyes on an Italian, but they were void of life. We studied each other in silence for a moment.

"Do you have any questions?"

"No, sir. I was just thanking your wife for this opportunity."

"I'm sure you will serve this family well, Juanita. You can start tomorrow. You will be expected to stay here. Will that be a problem?"

"No, I expected as much."

My pulse was racing the entire ride back to my safe house. My handler should be waiting when I get there.

"Hey, Juanita," Abby, my next-door neighbor, was outside playing with her son when I pulled up.

"How did it go?" Eric was sitting at my kitchen table, going through some paperwork.

"I start tomorrow," I fist-bumped him. "I will be living in their house as well."

"Juanita, I know this is a career-breaking case for you. You need to be careful! The Saccone's are dangerous people."

"I know, Eric. Could you not rain on my parade?"

"I'm just looking out for you. That's all."

"I know. I got this!"

"I hope so."

*　　　*　　　*

My first couple of weeks flew by at the Saccone Mansion. It was your run-of-the-mill cleaning and cooking.

When I could, I would snoop around to see if I could find something. I haven't observed anything that would warrant a wiretap yet. As soon as I got one, I was prepared to get them all over this house.

"You need to tell him that he needs to call before popping up at our home Neri," Elenor complained as she stormed into the kitchen.

I quickly poured her a glass of white wine. I'd at least learned that much about her.

"I can't speak to my father in that way. You know this, Elenor."

"Okay, I'll say something to him, honey," the sarcasm was her second language.

"Elenor."

"What? It's not my fault he's still pissed you married a black woman. He didn't calculate that my father would cut me off, did he? He thought he was going to get access to some new connections," she giggled. "Nope, just got stuck with me as a daughter-in-law," she took a big gulp from her goblet.

"Don't antagonize him."

"I'll be upstairs. I'm not in the mood for Luca's crap today. Don't take long getting rid of him. It's almost dinner time."

"I don't take orders from you, love."

"It's cute that you think that," she smirked before disappearing upstairs.

"I thought you were going to take care of that problem, Neri?" Luca Saccone was enraged as he walked into the kitchen.

"It's being handled."

"No! Handle it now!"

I could see Neri's temples throbbing. I quickly lowered my head over the sink as I pretended to wash the dishes. I did my best to look like I'm not paying attention.

"Juanita, please excuse us," Neri asked.

" Absolutely, Mr. Saccone."

I disappeared from the room but not out of hearing distance.

"It's not Elenor leaking information to the Feds dad! I'm still looking into it, but it's not her!"

How do they know we're getting information on them unless we have a mole?

I sent a quick text to my handler for a meeting. Neri was right. His wife wasn't the one working with us; it was his brother.

CHAPTER TWO

NERI SACCONE

Five Years Later

"Juanita, help him get the body inside the bag."

I sipped on my cognac as she and Abra, my second in command, struggled to get the dirty cop tucked away.

"I called the cleaning crew. They will be here shortly, Senior Saccone," Juanita huffed as she helped Abra.

Juanita had proven to be trustworthy and loyal. This was one of many bodies she has helped to hide. Juanita oversaw late dinners and countless meetings. I had started to trust Juanita more than Abra. She knew things my wife didn't know.

I couldn't wait until she was done so I could ravish her body. Something about watching her handle that dead body turned me on. She always recommended someone else or gave me a plan that kept me from getting my hands dirty.

"They're here. Abra, you ride with them."

"Okay, boss."

Once everyone was gone, I led Juanita into my office at the slaughterhouse. I adored my wife, but Juanita brought a passion I'd been longing for. She didn't look at me like a monster or like my father's flunky. She respected me as a man.

"We need to get back to the house," I told her after we'd had our fill of one another.

"I'm tired of stolen moments. I hate seeing Elenor with you!"

"I know. You know she is my wife and what that means in this family. If I could divorce her, I would, but I can't. Besides, she pregnant. I finally have my heir."

"She's what?"

"Juanita, she's my wife! Don't be naive. What we have will outlast the test of time but only if you trust me."

"How can I trust you when all I see you doing is living a lie? I serve you both like a slave while you screw me in dark corners and empty hallways. You don't love me! Take me home! Oh, excuse me. Take me home, Senior Saccone," her tears washed away her flawless make-up.

"Is that baby even yours?"

"What is that supposed to mean?" I closed the space between us with two large steps.

"You know exactly what I mean. You're not blind. Why do you think Elenor could care less if you stay out late or not?"

"You know you're not to speak on my wife, Juanita."

"Tuh," she scoffed before slamming the door to the car.

Her red lipstick was smeared all over her face and my body from our love-making session.

I cleaned myself up and did what she asked. When Juanita, Adra, and I left on late nights like this, Elenor knew not to ask too many questions.

"You have my heart, Juanita."

"But she has your name and soon your child Neri. I'm nothing but a nasty little secret."

"That's not tr-"

Before I could finish, she jumped out of the car and went inside.

"I'm glad you both made it back safely. Where is Adra?" Elenor asked.

"He had to wrap everything up. He'll be along soon."

"I know it's late, Juanita, but can you finalize the menu for the dinner party tomorrow. I made my changes and put notes for you to follow."

"Of course you did," Juanita rolled her eyes.

"Excuse me?" My wife walked up on her. "I don't know what your problem is, but you will not speak to me in that manner in my home. My husband may be familiar with you, but I'm not! Now, do as I asked you without the added attitude."

Juanita held her tongue while I held my breath. I knew what the underlying tension was about. I wasn't about to reveal that to my wife under any circumstances.

"I don't know what's gotten into her lately. Whenever I say something to her, she always has something smart to say or doesn't do it. You need to get her in check! I know she's been around for five years, and you trust her to do **things,** but I won't tolerate disrespect from your whore, Neri. I deal with enough of that from your father," her emphasis on things let me know she knew exactly why Juanita's panties were in a bunch.

"I'm sorry, baby. I'll handle it, *mia amata*," I promised her.

"You know everything has to be up to par. I already have to work twice as hard because I'm black."

"You handle them just fine," I assured her.

"What wrong? Is something that happened tonight bothering you?"

"No, is this baby mine Ellie?"

Her face hardened, but she knew I was well within my right to ask her this question. Due to my indiscretion with Juanita, I turned a blind eye to what I saw brewing between her and Dasante.

My father may want to bring him into the fold, but it would never happen. Not over my dead body.

"I told you that was over."

"Is it? Because you act like you can't stand the sight of me."

"Why would I compete with your affection when you no longer need anything from me. You can't blame me for wanting to be wanted by someone."

"I guess just anyone would do, huh?" I asked.

"That's not fair, Neri! The only reason that woman is still working here is that she knows too much to let her go, thanks to you! Do you know what she can do to you? To our family? If you cross her, there's not telling what damage she could do before your able to take her out!"

"We've made a mess of this, haven't we?"

"Yes, we did," she sighed. "You have my heart, Neri. You must know that."

"I know that you look at Dasante the way you use to look at me when we first got married. Maybe because he's black, is it that he can understand you in a way that I never could?"

"That's not true. Dasante just knows what it's like being black in a room full of Italians who don't want you there."

"You know what this was when you married me. You lucky I haven't killed Dasante."

"It's not for the lack of trying, Neri. You don't think he knows it was you that cut his break line?"

"That was a warning. If I wanted Dasante dead, he would be. If it weren't for my father's protection, this would go another way. Dasante Charles wants everything I got!"

Elenor was silent as I ranted. On the outside, it looked like we had it all together. Like she had me wrapped around her finger. I loved her, but that's not why she had my devotion. She found out about my detailed plan to kill my father. That went against everything the Bloody Five Stood for.

The Bloody Five were five mafia families who merged back in the eighties to secure power and wealth.

My father found a way to defraud the government out of gasoline tax. He was bringing in $320,000 a week as he started to distribute to local gas stations around the city of Houston.

It quickly rose to eight to ten million a week. Luca Saccone sold to branded and unbranded gas stations.

That's how he secured his spot as the Boss of Bosses of the Bloody Five. We weren't paying taxes to get the gas, so it was a tremendous profit.

From there, we got into construction through the labor unions and threatening work foremen and CEOs. We did whatever was required.

I never thought I would see the day my love for Elenor would falter. I know I drove her there and can even deal with the revenge. She fell in love with Dasante; that was something I couldn't forgive.

"Neri," Elenor pulled me from my thoughts. "Let's get to bed. We have a long day tomorrow preparing for the dinner. Please shower before getting into our bed. The smell of her is all over you."

A quick dip of my head let Elenor know that I understood.

* * *

"Thank you all for coming to celebrate with us. Many of you know the challenges we've faced within our family. Our love has produced an heir to our throne."

My father was the happiest I had seen him in a long time. He didn't care that Elenor was black for the time being. He was glad to have a grandchild on the way. Even if it was a girl, he had decided to train her up just the same. He felt she would be more deadly due to his belief that women were way more vicious than men.

Elenor glowed as the love poured in from the families. She was finally feeling accepted. Dasante's lust was evident all over his face. I could feel my temper rise.

After dinner, we convened to another area of the house where some could smoke, and others could have their fill of my cognac and red wine.

I was in deep conversation with Rimando Rufio when I noticed Elenor was not in the room. He's been trying to join our family, but my father was against it. He called the Rufino's bottom feeders. They never wanted to make any real sacrifices to show their allegiance to the Bloody Five.

"Excuse me, Rimando. I'll be right back," I high stepped out of the room to find my wife.

Juanita was searing my soul with her evil stares all night.

"You need to make a choice Elenor! You can't keep running back and forth!"

"It's not like you're going to leave your pregnant wife either! What, you're going to neglect your child to raise mine? I thought not!"

"You know the way that you love me runs deeper in your veins than the love you can ever have for Neri. He will never understand you as I do. How can he? He doesn't know what we deal with. How much harder we have to work to be just as good! To get what we deserve! I'm takin' scraps from his daddy just to get a stool at the table. Not even a seat because they don't respect me! I can't risk everything I'm doing for you, and you're not all in! I won't let you keep me from having the money and power I deserve."

"Well, it sounds like you've made my choice for me," she sighed. "Don't worry. Your secret is safe with me. I won't tell Neri about your lil' plan," she scoffed.

"Don't threaten me, Elenor! I'm not the one!"

"Yeah, yeah," she snaked her tongue down his throat.

I saw a side of my wife I didn't know existed—the disrespect of meeting with her lover at our dinner party to announce the arrival of our child.

"After this, you're dead to me!" He raised her dress up as I watched his hands disappear under her clothing.

I pulled my Smith & Wesson .38 caliber Model 10 revolver with the pearl grip from my holster, "You think you can disrespect me in my own house? My father said you were a whore! And I told him you couldn't be trusted, Dasante!"

"Who do you think put me on her? Your father was sure that her loyalty wasn't with your family Neri. He knew this would be the only way you would believe it."

"What? You were using me?"

"I was doing my job, Elenor! My loyalty is to Mr. Saccone. Even if he doesn't allow me at his table, he's shown me how to build my own," he walked away, leaving her standing there dumfounded. "You father wants to meet with us first thing in the morning," he stopped near me on his way out.

I still had a mind to shoot him where he stood, but instead, I nodded as he walked by me back to the party.

"You thought he loved you more than me? I did wrong but come on, Elenor. My father knows about what you've been doing. There's nothing I can do for you at this point."

"What is that supposed to mean, Neri?" She screamed.

I left her standing there exposed. I knew what the meeting with my father would be about in the morning. After she gave birth to my child, I would have to get rid of her.

I was conflicted about it all.

"Are you okay?" Juanita stopped me in the dark hallway.

"Yes, I love you so much! Thank you for sticking by my side and being loyal. From this day forward, things will be different. I promise.

CHAPTER THREE

ELENOR SACCONE

Ten Years Later

I thought I would've been dead by now. When Neri's father, Luca Saccone, died, I felt like I could finally breathe. I knew they were only waiting until I had my daughter to off me.

Once he died, I knew there was no way Neri would kill me. Despite how much he despised me, he could never kill the mother of his child.

I've been teaching Averly as much as I could about her culture, about me, and my side of the family. I doubt if Neri will make sure she remembers.

Neri didn't pull me from the slums. I'm a mob princess in my own right. My father runs the Westside of Chicago. Too bad I hate his guts. I'd rather die than ask him for help. Long as my baby girl is safe, that's all that matters.

"Can I get you anything?" Juanita asked.

Over the years, we made peace with what this was. Juanita was now the woman who had Neri's heart.

Little did she know that she could never compete with his love for the Saccone empire.

"You can do one thing for me. If anything happens to me, I need you to take care of Averly Grace like she's your daughter Juanita."

"You will be around Elenor Saccone."

"Juanita, you can stop. We both know what this is. I just need you to at least be honest in this moment to ensure me Averly will always have you no matter what! I don't care if you end up not working here. You find a way to watch over my daughter!"

She was silent as she considered what I was asking of her. I knew she would because Averly was an extension of Neri. She adored that man.

"I will give my life if I must to keep her safe, Elenor. I promise."

"Thank you."

"Now that his father is dead, you know there is no danger anymore," she sat next to me as if we were friends.

"I'm not so sure. I have this feeling in my gut that something is off Juanita. I've made my peace with my choices, but I worry about leaving my baby girl alone with Neri. He can be cold at times. I don't want her hard like them, Juanita. I don't want him to ruin her."

"I won't let him. I promise. I hope you're wrong. I know we don't see eye to eye, but I don't want anything to happen to you. If I hear anything, I will let you know."

"Thank you, Juanita."

We both knew she was lying. She would never betray Neri. Juanita was gone over him. The things she's done in the name of loving him, I would never do. That made it easier for him to fall in love with her. I'm not hiding bodies or witnessing murders.

My father kept that life from me. I wasn't about to start jeopardizing my life to please my husband.

That's how I met Neri. My father was their supplier for years until they found a better one.

My father was possessive of my mother and me. Neri was my way out. I didn't love him like that but eventually fell for him.

Maybe Juanita was right. I could just be worried for no reason.

* * *

I dreaded going to my mammogram appointment today. The techs put you in that thin robe while you stand in a cold room as they squeeze your boobie for dear life.

"Juanita, I'll be back after my appointment."

"Okay, I have, Averly," she smiled.

"I love you, mama," Averly ran up, wrapping her arms around my waist.

"I love you more munchkin," I pulled her close and kissed her all over her face.

Normally, I tossed my purse on the passenger seat of the Porsche before I got in. My fitted skirt made that nearly impossible.

My chest heaved up and down once I was inside from being out of breath.

This car sat so low, but I looked good in it. Once I turned the car on, I noticed the tire pressure light was on.

I looked down at my watch, then back up at the light. I didn't have time for one of the drivers to pull another car around from the garage.

I shrugged it off and heading to my appointment. I merged onto Interstate 45, so I could head downtown.

Boom!

My car started to spin out of control after I heard the loud noise. My heart was beating so fast I thought it would detonate in my chest.

Everything was a blur due to the blood blinding me until I heard my other tires trying to grip the highway. Sharp pains were assassinating every part of my body.

Skkkrttt!

Boom!

CHAPTER FOUR

JUANITA ALVAREZ

"Neri Saccone, how could you?" I screamed through the tears that poured from my eyes.

I was hurt that Eleanor died in the car crash, but I was devastated about what this would do to Averly Grace.

"Keep your voice down! Averly doesn't know yet! I had nothing to do with this! My father assured me that he called off the hit before he died!"

"He lied! Elenor's death is going to break your daughter into tiny pieces!"

"I know," he dissolved into tears.

I believed that he didn't have anything to do with her death. Even from the grave, Luca Saccone was damaging this family.

He was a vile man who deserved worse than to die from a heart attack on the toilet. Scumbag.

"I have to tell Averly Grace before she sees it on the news."

"I know you killed my daughter!" A six-foot-five-man stormed through the front door.

"How did you get onto my property, Kentrell!" Neri spat.

"I told you if I wanted to get to you, I could any time I wanted. I know you were behind my daughter's death!"

"I would never hurt her, Kentrell!"

"Mommy is dead?" Averly Grace walked up behind us. None of us noticed she had come into the room."

"Oh, baby," Neri rushed over to her.

"I want my mama," she screamed while punching her dad in the chest. "I need my mama!"

Her cry made the entire room standstill.

"That's my grandbaby?" Kentrell asked.

"Yes, this will be the only time you will ever lay eyes on her. Get him out of here," Neri ordered his security team.

"One way or another, I'm getting my grandbaby, Neri Saccone. You watch!" He threatened before being escorted out.

That was the first and only time I ever saw Eleanor's father.

CHAPTER FIVE

JUANITA ALVAREZ

Present Day

I quickly wiped away the single tear that escaped my eye as I waited for Lexington to decide how he wanted to proceed. I loved Averly as my own, but there was also a pang of guilt behind my caring for her.

I was the one reporting back to the Feds, but Luca suspected his son and Elenor as the snitches. That's what made him use Dasante to set her up.

I stuck to my promise. I raised Averly like she was my own.

"You've been allowing my wife to cry in your arms and love you like a mother all the while you're Fed?"

I gripped my trigger tighter as Lexington rushed towards me.

"Give me one good reason not to body you right now!"

"I already have mine. You have to get to yours. Listen, this is not black and white. I love Averly! I don't care about this job more than her. You tell me the play! If we are dropping bodies, I'm helping you hide them. It's up now. It's taken them over twenty years to build this case. They're not just after the Saccone's. It's all the entire Bloody Five and now your father. When you married Averly, they wanted him as well. The FBI feels like they need to take them all down at once to kill the organization once and for all."

"You lay this on me while my wife is missing? We trusted you!"

"I'm sorry, but it's about to hit the fan. My confession is my last-ditch effort to save you all. Hopefully, Neri will realize this is what's best."

"I know you are not telling him this?"

"Not yet. We need to get Averly back safely. I wanted to talk to you. I can use my other resources at the Bureau, but it's going to be a different ball game altogether. They'll try to use it to their advantage."

"Let me see if Reno can find her. If not, then do what you must."

"I understand completely. I'll use some favors first to get as far as I can."

"Okay," his response was weak and helpless.

CHAPTER SIX

LEXINGTON CHARLES

I dawdled for a while, alone in Averly's empty old room we shared before we got married. I pulled her black satin robe from the hook on the back of the door and inhaled her residue. I was infuriated by my helplessness.

"Hold on for me, baby. I'm coming. I promise!" I went limp as I buried my face in the pillow on her side of the bed.

I tossed and turned all last night. I know my baby can take care of herself, but it's my job to protect her. I failed her like everyone else in her life. I didn't bother praying this morning because I needed a face-to-face with my pastor. I needed to repent prematurely for the hell I was about to unleash. Whoever has my wife and unborn child, I would make sure gets delivered to the pearly gates.

Wait until Averly finds out about Juanita being a Fed. She's going to lose it. She loves that woman like a mother.

I knocked on my pastor's door and waited for him to invite me in.

"Lexington. So good to see you. What is troubling you, son? You sounded unsettled on the phone."

"Yes, my wife is missing. The way that I'm going to handle it, I just need you to send a prayer up for me."

He eyed the length of my body as he folded his hand in a steeple.

"You don't trust the authorities to handle it?"

"Pastor Tucker, you know what my family is into. We didn't bother to get the authorities involved, but we're working on getting her home."

"The authorities have way more resources than your clan does, Lexington. Your wife's life is more important than any attention you fear bringing to your father's doorstep."

"I'm not under his thumb anymore, Pastor. When I married my wife, she showed me that I could be my own man. It's simpler working to make her happy than my father. Nothing I do is good enough for him, but my wife appreciates everything I do. She has proven to have my back when it's down to the wire. She has easily become my favorite person on this earth," I beamed with pride.

"Wow. I know how important it was for you for so many years to have your father's approval. Keep down this path, Lexington. He won't like it in the end once he realizes it, but see this through. Just because he's your father, that doesn't give him the right to demean you or make you feel unworthy. Continue to set healthy boundaries as you build your own family. You don't need that poison spilling over into the life you're building with your wife. You deserve to be happy. I'll be praying for your wife's safe return and that you won't have to do anything that will keep you up at night."

I liked the way he put that. There is no way I'd feel bad about obliterating anyone that threatened the safety and sanity of my wife.

"Thank you for your prayers and encouragement, Pastor Tucker."

"Always a pleasure. I'm sure you will get your wife back safe and sound. When things settle, please bring her to a Sunday service."

"You have my word. Consider it done."

Once I made it to my car, I noticed I had a missed call from Juanita. I pressed the green button to return her call.

"You called?" I asked when she answered. Juanita was the opp now, so she deserved every bit of attitude I was dishing.

"I got something. The traffic cameras have them driving two hours out, and then they lose track because they're no cameras that far out."

"Man!" I yelled, swerving slightly out of my lane when I smashed my fist against the steering wheel.

"Wait. I was still able to run the plates. They came back registered to an Antonio Rufino. Averly turned down his proposal years ago. I know he's not still feeling slighted from her rejection?" She said.

"Nah, it's something else."

"What?" She pried.

"I'll tell you later. Thanks for the info. I'll keep you posted. I'm going to my father's to see if they have found out anything from the streets."

"Okay. Keep me posted. I'm still digging on this end too."

"Thanks, Juanita."

"Of course."

I didn't forget either that she was about to up her pistol on me at the house.

I haven't been able to stay at our home without Averly. I've been at the Saccone mansion. I didn't go to my father's because I don't think I could hide my anger if he says something out the way about Avery.

I loved my wife, but I just haven't figured out a way to tell my father. That may not be an issue for much longer. On top of my wife missing, we're still under pressure to kill our parents by the Rufino family.

I couldn't think about that right now, though. Averly is my only priority.

Why would Tonio just take her when they gave us both the ultimatums, though? It wasn't adding up.

Now that I know who's behind this, I can turn up the heat. I don't care about any of that organization crap either. I'm disrespecting any and everybody about mine.

As bad as I wanted to just run up on Tonio and his daddy, I knew I couldn't. I had to be smart. I'm no good to my wife and child if I'm dead.

I know we haven't gotten a DNA test, but I know that child is mine. I can feel it in my bones.

I bent the corner to my father's house. Finding out Tonio was behind this made me think my dad may have an alternate plan in place. I was hoping when he found out she was pregnant that would buy me some time, but I guess not.

I blew past the workers and henchman as I quickly closed in on the space that stood between my father's office and me.

I barged in with a firm grip on my Colt .38 that I had modified to shoot full auto with an extended magazine capability and a Thompson grip.

I held his gaze for a moment with my gun pressed firmly between his eyes, "Call the mafia together today! If my wife gets killed because of you, I'm going to lose it! You told me days ago you would find out something. I haven't heard anything from you!"

His eyes were stormy. My disrespect had pissed him off, "Why are you so upset? This could be working out in our favor. We planned to kill her and her father anyway."

"Did you forget she's carrying the heir?" I swiftly played it off.

"Your right. The Saccone bloodline is still represented in that child. I'll get our people together. In the meantime, what are you going to do?"

"I'm going to talk to Neri and see if I can find out some additional information. I'll have him round up the other families as well. We need all hands on deck. She's been gone too long. Each day decreases the chances of us finding her alive."

When I left my father's office, he was on the phone. I knew he could care less about my baby surviving. It was only the reminder of how tighter his grip of power would be with it.

Whatever works for him to help me get them back. I would figure everything else out after that.

I cut across three lanes of traffic, careening over the medium to speed back in the other direction. I jammed my car into gear and gunned the engine. The vehicle-mounted the curve as I swerved into the circle drive in front of the Saccone mansion.

I was hoping Neri could remember something that would lead to where my wife was.

CHAPTER SEVEN

AVERLY GRACE

"Say, man! This water is too hot!" I snorted with derision. "How am I supposed to wash this funk off me if my skin is going to melt off?"

"Look, stop complaining. You lucky we even bathed you, my nigga."

"My nigga? You act like you never loved me, Grecia. How can you watch this man treat me this way?"

"It was easy once I realized how easy it was for you to walk out on me and up and marry someone you didn't know."

"Tonio planted you in my life! You never loved me, so stop capping like you a scorned lover when you're not! I thought you were some kind of boss when the whole time you just a flunky. What happened to we don't lie to each other? Ever! That's the rule!"

"Watch ya' mouth before I choke you out again, Averly. You know I can't stand that smart mouth of yours. You'll make a nigga put their hands on you for real."

"Only a weak nigga put his hands on a woman."

"Yeah, whatever. Just get in the tub," Grecia nudged me. "Hurry up and hit what needs to be washed. You have a doctor's appointment to get to."

"What doctor's appointment?"

"Tonio said something about getting your placenta tested to see if I'm the pappy," he joked.

"I'm glad this is a joke to you."

"She still ain't ready?" Tonio barged into the bathroom. I quickly covered my body. I didn't care about Grecia seeing me because he's been all over every inch of it. Tonio dusty self could never lay eyes on all of this.

"What do y'all think this is going to be if Grecia is the father? Some weird thruple?"

"I haven't really thought about it," Grecia said. "I mean, we might as well since I still have love for you."

I sucked my teeth at his lies.

"I could learn to love you," Tonio leaned in like he was going to kiss me.

Smack!

"Nigga I wish you would!" I bit down on my lip so hard I could taste blood.

He just laughed, "You better be glad I don't hit females."

"You better be glad I don't have my pistol!" I threatened.

Smack!

"But I do," Grecia's hand was so quick I didn't see it coming.

"Nigga what you do that for? She can't be going in there with no bruises on her. They gone ask questions. You better hope that doesn't leave no mark!"

"I'm going to peel the skin off both of y'all after I cut your vocal cords so you can't scream," I spat through clenched teeth. "Lexington and I are going to kill you slowly. What happened to your father telling us we had to kill our parents and allow The Rufino's into the organization?"

"He was taking too long. My plan is much better."

"Look at it this way, instead of one baby daddy, you will now have two," he was smiling so hard his eyeballs were barely visible. "Plot twist, if the baby isn't mine, we're killing it."

His word felt like someone's fingernails were ripping into my gut. I didn't see things going this far left. Man, I honestly didn't think it would take Lexington this long to find me.

If I were in the city, I knew he would be able to with no problem. I figured I was out in the country because I never hear people, traffic, or anything other than birds. I must figure out a way to save myself before these niggas kill my baby and me.

"I still remembered your style," Grecia handed me the clothes like he just didn't put hands on me.

"Ugghh!" Grecia grunted as my foot connected with the place where his balls should be. Tonio had them in his pocket.

"Nigga you gone learn about putting your hands on me!" I launched a loogie at his face.

I put the clothes on, he laid on the counter, and rushed out of the bathroom, "Not so fast. Don't get any ideas at this office, or you're going to get a bunch of innocent people killed. Understand?" Tonio warned me.

"I understand."

The slice of light through the door expanded and cut across the entrance. I was just glad to see something other than the four walls in the basement.

My gaze sifted them like a handful of pebbles.

"Blindfold her so we can go," he instructed Grecia.

He was still fuming from the blow I dealt to his nut sack.

"That'll teach him," I chuckled out.

He brutally tied the piece of fabric around my eyes, "It's too tight!"

"Man, didn't I tell you she can't show up with no bruises. Nigga you act really slow sometimes. That's why you can never move up. You are led too easily by your emotions. You making this personal, and this is strictly business."

"You want to make sure she can't see or not? Nigga stop talking to me like a child."

Tonio dismissed him with a wave of a hand I saw while Grecia was adjusting my blindfold.

"He be punking you," I teased.

"Mind your business. I can't wait to kill you on my soul," he grunted.

He dragged me outside to the car. I could hear the door open. Grecia roughly stuffed me inside.

"Don't do anything stupid in this doctor's office," Tonio warned again. "I'm not afraid to kill a pregnant woman. I know you don't see it now, but all of this is for the best."

"Who are you to decide what's best for me?"

Tonio didn't bother answering before blasting his music. I hate it here.

CHAPTER EIGHT

JUANITA ALVAREZ

I secreted my resignation letter away in the pocket of my uniform as I glided towards Neri. My insides quivered with fear. He's been irritated lately with Averly missing. We've all been on edge, but I couldn't hide any longer who I was. It was as if I could sense every nerve, cell, muscle, drop of blood, and hair in and on my body individually. I pushed open the door to his office. He was deep in thought as the weight I had gained over twenty years put the creaky floorboards in a complaining mood as I crossed the darkened office.

"What are you doing to find her?" I demanded.

"Everything humanly possible! What do you think?"

"I found a car that left the scene from traffic cameras in the area. I was able to follow them up until they got about two hours outside the city. The car is registered to an Antonio Rubio?"

"Rubio? Are you certain? Wait. How do you know this?"

I was cemented in place by fear and turmoil. I wanted to lay my truth at his feet and prayed he would still love me, but I doubt it. Neri doesn't take betrayal lightly.

"Why are you sitting behind this desk instead of sending the city up in flames to help me look for my wife?" Lexington closed the space between him and Neri so fast he caught us both off guard.

"Get your hands off me!" Neri pressed his gun against Lexington's groin, who returned the favor with a firearm to Neri's temple.

"Son, I know you're scared. This is not the way we're going to find her. I have all the families with their ears to the streets, but no one is talking!"

"Then make them talk! Are you the boss of bosses or not?" He screamed.

Fury blew from him like a high-powered fan as he loosened his grip on Neri.

"I just filled him in on what I found out as well," I interjected."

"Is that so? Did you also tell him how you were privy to said information?"

My eyes pleaded with Lexington to let me do this my way, but my pleas were null and void.

"She was about to before you came in here acting like a maniac."

The room was quiet as both their eyes fell on me.

"I'm a federal agent Neri."

"Bwwhahhaha!" He fell to his seat as tears filled his eyes from laughing so hard. "Now is not the time for this foolishness."

"Neri, I'm telling the truth," my words were just as minced as my emotions. I tossed my badge on the desk. All the color drained from his face when he realized it wasn't a joke.

"You slither into my home under the guise of a servant-"

"And lover, I reminded him."

"Didn't see that one coming, but it makes sense now," Lexington added his unwanted commentary.

With one swoop, Neri gripped my throat so tight my breathing was constricted, "You played me for some fool?" He asked as his gun cut into my forehead. "My wife was killed because my father thought she was the one giving intel to the Feds!"

His breathing was labored, but his eyes revealed his heartbreak was ripping raw inside out.

"Go ahead. I'm not afraid to die. You will have to explain your action to Averly Grace! She will hate you even more! Do you dare take another mother from her? Or the Feds will run in here to carry you off for taking my life."

"So it's true? You killed her mama Neri?" Lexington acted shocked that the whispers in the streets were true. During roundtable meetings in dark corners, the gossip spat was confirmed as they danced off Neri's lips.

"It's complicated," he huffed, loosening his grip on me.

"Complicated? You took her mother from her!" Lexington was outraged by the pain his wife was forced to suffer at the hands of her father.

I was relieved that he had grown to love her truly. She would need someone once I am gone to take care of her. She thinks she strong, which she is, but she needs someone that her heart is safe with.

"I'm the only one who has the key to your freedom Neri," I offered him a way out.

"How am I supposed to trust anything you say?"

"Just as I have trusted you within these walls year after year. One bad decision after another that landed you on the doorstep of Dasante Charles's after what he did to you and Elenor."

"Don't act like her being out of the way didn't benefit you! You were in my bed the same night, spreading your legs from the East to the West for me. You laid in the spot that was still drenched with the smell of her perfume."

"You professed your love for me long before that! Don't put what you did on me!"

"Look, we don't have time for this! With every passing moment, my wife could be out there fighting for her life! If they find out my child is not Grecia's, they could kill it! I'm not losing either of them! Neri, I need you to think! Where would Tonio take Averly that two hours outside the city?"

He rubbed his salt and pepper beard as he pondered my question.

"They have an old farmhouse out that way if I recall correctly from back in the day. Heinous acts were performed out there. I'm sure it still smells of death."

"My father has assembled a team to help. Let the other members the families have assigned to find my wife know what's going on," he was barking commands at Neri like he was the boss.

"I promise you we will get her back safely. Once we do, please allow me to tell her the truth about her mother," Neri pleaded with Lexington.

"I don't care about anything but my wife's safety. You better hope for your sake she and my unborn child is alive."

"Careful, son."

"I don't have to be careful!"

"You will watch your tone standing in my home. I'm still the boss of bosses, so what I say goes! I've shown you more love and compassion than your father has. I've known you all for many years. I've witnessed how his envy of you makes him lash out to break you down. With every year, you grow more and more into the man he could never be, and he hates you for it."

"My father loves me. Don't speak on what you don't understand," he stammered.

"I understand more than you know. I don't pity envy, fear, or hate you, Lexington Charles. I am growing to love you like a son. We will find Averly. Together! Knowing what I know about Juanita, I'm relieved she will have you once this is all over."

Lexington didn't say anything. As if we all understood what we needed to do next, we headed out. The three people who loved Averly most were on their way to avenge those who violated her.

CHAPTER NINE

AVERLY GRACE

"Look, stop tweaking!" Tonio rammed his unnoticeable twenty-two into my back. His words grew legs, kicked me in my chest, and drove all the breathable air from my body.

I drew in a shallow breath and attempted to get my body to do as he insisted.

"Hey, how you doin'?" Grecia flashed his mouth full of golds to the receptionist, who immediately perked up like her meal ticket had just walked in.

"How can I help you, sir?" She licked her full lips.

"Yes, my baby mama here for an appointment."

"Oh," her attitude shifted. "What's her name and date of birth?"

Grecia rattled off my information which wasn't a shock. He always made a big deal out of my birthdays. I don't even know what was real or if any of it was.

"Okay, I have her checked in."

"Can you let the staff know my homeboy is going to be coming back as well? Yeah, either of us could be the father. You know how that can go."

The girl flashed me a side-eye like I was so slut bustin' it open for anyone who paid attention to me.

"I'll tell them. It should be fine."

"Thank you, love."

The waiting room was empty, but inside I prayed for an opportunity for me to get away.

"Avery Grace Saccone," the nurse called my name as she held a firm grip on her clipboard.

I stood up and followed her to the back.

"Let me have you stop here so I can get your weight."

I did as she asked while she scribbled the results on her sheet of paper.

"Here, before we draw your blood, I need a urine sample."

"Okay," I told her.

Tonio went to follow me in the restroom, "Can she get a little privacy? It's already hard to pee on demand," the nurse intervened.

"Grecia, I'll go out to the waiting room," Tonio smacked his lips.

"Okay," he agreed.

"It's going to be the first door on the left," she rolled her eyes.

"There are cups in there already. Once you're done, pull the small silver door open and place your sample inside."

"Okay," my head bounced up and down.

"Are you okay?"

Grecia was leaning against the door, watching me, "Yes, I'm fine, just getting used to being pregnant. This is my first appointment," I lied.

"You're in good hands. I promise. I'm Alishia. I'll be your nurse today," she smiled, ushering me in the bathroom. "I'll get the sample when you're done."

"Okay."

The tiny plastic cup was an easy task with my full bladder. It quickly warmed from my pee.

My pee smelled like ammonia from the malnourishment. I placed the cup in the slot as instructed.

When the body leaned over, I could see Alisha's name tag through the opening.

"I've been kidnapped," I sobbed.

"For real? You want me to call the police?"

"God no! That will only make it worse. Just let me go, please."

"Hold up. Let me make sure they took the big one to get his blood drawn."

I sat back on the toilet with my pants still around my ankles. Just in case Grecia barged in, I wanted to make it seem like I was still trying to pee.

In a matter of minutes, Alishia was back, "The Italian one still in the lobby flirting with our receptionist. The big one is getting his blood drawn. I gave him a thick questionnaire to fill out too. I told him it was for the DNA test. What do you want to do? I can get you out the back door and hold them off as long as I can. Here, take my phone."

"Are you sure?"

"Girl, yes! If you can't call the police, I'm sure you have your reasons as to why. I won't rest unless I know you're at least able to call someone to help you! I haven't been able to charge it, so make it count, boo."

"Thank you so much."

"Okay, I'm going to make sure the door to your room is closed. If it is, I'll knock softly on the door twice very quickly."

"Okay."

She disappeared, and the next sound I heard was the two quick taps on the door.

I snatched my leggings up and briskly walked out of the bathroom. None of the other nurses were the wiser to me and Alishia's plan.

We passed a break room loitered with food on the tables. It looked like they were having a potluck.

She caught me looking, "Girl, I don't trust these people's food. Probably have cats sitting on the counter for all I know, chile."

As promised, once we passed the time clock, I was at the back exit.

"Call for help!" She shoved her phone into the palm of my hand.

"Thank you so much!" I threw my arms around her neck before running as fast as I could in the opposite direction towards the gas station I saw on the way here.

As I ran, I quickly punched Lexington's number. I called over and over, but each time he ignored my call. He didn't know the number, but you would think that he would answer any number that popped up! Men could be idiots sometimes!

My body locked up with rage, but it didn't paralyze my stride. The battery icon was flashing red. The phone was about to die, and I was running out of options.

I quickly sent Lexington a text.

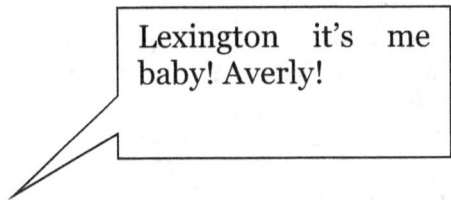

Lexington it's me baby! Averly!

"Averly!" My heart melted as my name rolled off of my husband's tongue. But could he get to me in time?

CHAPTER TEN

LEXINGTON CHARLES

"So, was any of it real?" Neri badgered Juanita as we took the two-hour drive. Seven more black SUVs led and trailed us. Each filled with more guns than we could need.

"At first, it wasn't. I was just doing my job. There was no way to get to you without letting you in. I had to be vulnerable to you as well. When I fell in love with you, it made things...complicated. When I fell in love with Averly, it made things impossible. I stopped feeding them information on you, Neri. I've been giving them information about the other families. I've made it to where you can get out of this."

"There's no way out of this, Juanita. You know this to be true. The Bloody Five will erase the Saccone name with our blood."

"I just need you to trust me, Neri."

"What about my family Juanita? Did you do us dirty too?"

I looked down at my phone and pressed ignore on my phone. My full attention was on getting to my wife. I didn't need any distractions. Any business would have to wait.

"I was never investigating your family. When I came into the picture, your father was close with Neri's father, but he didn't have a major pull in the city yet. What I didn't know is that he's been silently building his empire. Whispering deals in dark corners of nightclubs and private villas in other countries. Your father has been busy, but no, he wasn't a part of the deal at first."

"At first?"

"It wasn't until your father merged with the Bloody Five that Dasante got on the Feds radar. No offense, but Italians don't care much for minorities if you get my drift."

"Yes, I get it. My father earned his seat at that table. After Neri's father died, the promises that were made were put to rest with him."

"That man doesn't deserve to rest," Neri mumbled.

"That we can agree on," Juanita and I chimed in unison.

I pressed ignore on the number again as I continued my line of questioning like I was the agent.

"So, is my father in danger of losing his freedom? What about Averly and me?"

"You and Averly will be safe. You have my word! Neri knows what he has to do," she glared at him.

I looked down at my phone and opened the message from the unknown number.

"It's Averly!"

Before I could call the number, it was ringing again, "Averly!"

"Lexington," she screamed bloody murder. "Baby, I need you to come and get me!"

"Where are you?"

"I'm not sure. I don't recognize the area! They're going to find me, Lexington!"

"Hold on, baby! I'm only about an hour out!"

"Every car that passes me makes my heart jump in my throat. I'll wait at this Valero gas station until you get here!" she cried.

Panic assailed me hearing her crying out in fear and not being able to help her.

"Drive faster! She's in trouble!" I yelled at Neri, who didn't hesitate to press down on the gas. "Averly! Averly!"

There was silence on the other end of the phone. Worry snaked through me like a virus. Regret fell on me like boulders from not answering the unknown number from the beginning.

Hopefully, they took her somewhere close in the area. If they were smart, they wouldn't venture too far from where they had her held up.

"What did she say?" Neri desperately asked.

"She said she had somehow escaped. She was running; it sounded like. I've never heard fear in Averly's voice, not once since I've known her."

"If she's scared, then it must be bad. We got to get to her!" Neri panicked.

Overcast skies turned everything dreary and cold. I took all my guns out and checked them again. My fave I would use on Tonio would be my butterfly knife. I'd plan to turn him into a eunuch and watch him bleed out.

"She's a fighter. She will be okay," Juanita tried to reassure us.

It was of no use. Averly's fire had been extinguished. The many layers I had to peel away were on full display. I don't know what Tonio had done to her, but she's broken.

I gripped my gun so tight my nails were digging into my palms. The stinging alerted me that I was bleeding.

I wiped my hands clean on my slacks. Neri was weaving in and out of traffic, trying to get to his daughter.

Neri was selfish, but at least he loved his daughter. His words replayed in my head of treating me better than my father had.

The words he spoke were the truth. Since being around Neri, he has taken the time to explain things to me that my father never did.

Neri treated me like a man instead of a walking mistake. Even now, I had little faith that his men would meet us there.

If he did, it would be because he would benefit in some way.

I didn't trust my father, but I have no idea what lies ahead for any of us now, knowing that Juanita is an agent.

I could care less. I just want my wife back in my arms safe. Ways that I would make Tonio pay haven't been invented yet.

His desperation to be a part of the Bloody Five reminded me of my father. People coveted this organization but had no idea what it took to be a part of it.

The sacrifices required of you go beyond just killing, robbing, embezzling, and whatever else they decide you should do.

You are expected to walk away from the life you built. Your life's purpose is to serve the cause of the empire.

Avery and I were called to duty to merge two families to form an alliance to ensure that peace is kept. Neri not only needed my father's money, but he also needed the army of men that's behind him.

My father's men were loyal to him and everything he stood for. He didn't know it, but they were more loyal to me than him. I was the one making sure they ate.

If it were up to my father, they would only have enough to survive. My father was greedy. He felt like everyone around him owed him something.

I treated our henchman like family. Yes, we were paying them, but paid loyalty could be changed. Your people must love you for them to fall on their swords for you.

They have to believe in you before they will die for your cause.

"There is the gas station. Pullover right here," I jumped out of the truck before it could stop. I was nearly run over. "Hey, did y'all see a pregnant woman that seemed nervous or was could've been running from somebody?"

People were afraid to respond.

"Two men grabbed her and drove off that way," a portly woman pointed North.

"Thank you so much!" Neri fell over when I turned around and bumped into him.

"What did you find out," he grunted as I pulled him from the oil-stained pavement.

"That lady said two guys grabbed her, and they headed North."

"Okay, let's go!"

CHAPTER ELEVEN

ANTONIO RUFINO

"Sir, calm down! I'm sure she's here somewhere," I heard a female's voice trying to calm Grecia's thundering yelling.

"Ma'am, is something wrong with the lady I just brought in for her appointment?" I asked the girl at the front desk who'd been flirting with me.

"They went to the bathroom to get her, and she was gone," she mumbled as if they had misplaced a toddler.

"What?" My bellowing voice rattled her.

"We need to go now!" Grecia burst through the doors and jogged by me.

Once we were outside, I grabbed him by the arm, "Grecia, what happened?"

"They took her to get a urine sample. I waited in the room. When I asked what was taking so long, they said something about maybe she was getting her blood drawn. I didn't think anything of it until the time kept passing. I went to knock on the bathroom door, and she was gone. The nurse said she must've slipped out one of the other exits."

"Man, you had one job!" Tonio complained. I would like him to see if he could keep tabs on her.

"What was I supposed to do? We already suspect with both of us coming in there with her! We are wasting time. Let's head back that way towards those stores."

I was barely in the car good before he peeled out of the parking lot of the doctor's office.

"She couldn't have gotten that far," I told him.

"You don't know Averly. That girl is stubborn and a fighter."

"If we don't find her, it's a wrap on our plan Grecia."

"You don't think I know that?"

"Look, is that her?" I pointed at a small, framed woman running in the opposite direction when she saw us.

"Yeah, that's Averly," with a hard jerk of the wheel to the left, he pulled into the gas station.

There were a few people pumping gas. We both pulled out our guns, took the safety off, and cocked them.

"Help! Help me please!" Averly's face was twisted in terror. People were afraid to get involved, so they quickly got into their cars.

She tried to run into the gas station, but they locked the doors on her, "We called the police to help you out!" The Indian attendant yelled through the glass as I snatched Averly up.

Wap! I hit Averly so hard my hand stung from the impact.

"If you ruined this for us, I will kill you and that bastard child of yours!" I spat.

"Man, we don't have time for this! Let's go!" Grecia pulled me off Averly.

The altercation had cleared the gas station. People didn't know how situations would escalate. They wanted no parts of being killed in the crossfire behind someone else's mess.

I drug her with the fistful of hair to the car.

"Let's get back to the spot now! We need to get our stuff packed up and get out of dodge. Ain't no telling who saw what or who she contacted!"

"Who did you call?" I smacked her around her some more.

"I want to see you lay your hands on my husband like that when he gets here! That's who I called. I'm going to make sure he peels your skin from your body faggot!"

Wap!

"Well, I'm going to beat you until he gets here!"

"Man, that's enough!" Grecia interjected.

"I know you didn't! You've been beating her for years now. Stop capping."

"Let's get her up out of here. Forget that stuff."

"Nah, we got laptops and burner phones there. We can't afford to leave anything behind."

"We got company," Grecia yelled, speeding through the stop sign, nearly getting us smashed by an eighteen-wheeler.

"Grecia, watch where you are going!"

Tak!

Tak!

Tak!

The black SUVs start unloading, trying to shoot out the tires. We bent down the red dirt road that led to the abandoned farmhouse.

Averly crouched on the floor behind Grecia's seat. "Yeah, they gone kill you for us. You know they all want you dead like you, mama, right?" I fired back at the SUVs.

Grecia drove us in the rotted-out wood barn.

"Hey, grab her!" I yelled to Grecia, who was busy returning fire to the fleet of vehicles that pulled up.

When he went to grab her, I noticed Lexington jump out of the truck. The nigga look like he was walking in slow motion. He must've thought he was bulletproof because his arm was raised blasting at Grecia.

Pop!

Pop!

Lexington put two bullets in Grecia's head. Averly never broke stride as she sprinted full force in his direction. She had complete faith that Lexington wouldn't let her get shot.

Once I noticed Grecia was dead, I ran out the back door of the garage. I had my Porsche hid a quarter of a mile down a nearby back road.

Pop!

Pop!

Pop!

Tak!

Tak!

Tak!

"Arrgghh!" I bellowed out in pain as the hot metal tore through my flesh.

I dipped into some nearby bushes and took the trail that led to my car. I pressed the unlock button and jumped inside.

Kssshh!

My back window shattered as one of the bullets violated it. I was grateful it didn't take my head off with it.

I kicked the Porsche into full power as I burned the road down to get back to the city. My father wasn't privy to my plan, but now that all hell has broken loose, I had to warn him about what I've done.

Had Averly not escaped, we would've got our spot at the table like we deserved and cleared our name.

I frantically looked behind me to see if I was still being followed, but I didn't see them.

"Where is my father?" I cried, bursting into the house.

"Tonio, what happened?" My mother's face was instantly soaked in tears.

"I'm fine, mom."

"Get the doctor here now before I have someone's head on a silver platter!" The servants began to scatter as I unleashed my anger on them.

"Tonio, who did this to you?" My dad ripped my sleeve to expose my wound. "It's just a flesh wound, for God's sake!"

"I had everything under control!"

"You had what under control?" My dad was confused.

"I kidnapped Averly Grace. I've had her this entire time held up at the old abandoned farmhouse. It was all going smoothly until she escaped when we took her to a doctor's appointment."

"What? I told you we had other plans!" My father was livid.

"Your plan was not working fast enough! You deserve to be at that table just as much as anyone else! Because of their lies, you were exiled from the Bloody Five!"

"You almost got yourself killed. I won't stand for Neri's constant disrespect of my family. He should've called me and allowed me the opportunity to handle this. I'm done with him thinking the Rufino family are worthless rats! Today we kill them all."

"No, I barely escaped Dasante Charles' gunman. If we can turn him, then we can wipe the Saccone's out once and for all. I've heard there are murmurs amongst the five about how he's been leading."

"Dasante was in cahoots with Neri blaming me for Elenor's death," my father squinted his eyes as if I didn't understand how deep his thirst for vengeance ran.

"We have to look at the bigger picture if you want to take Neri down and make him pay."

"You're right, Tonio. I'll set up a meeting."

CHAPTER TWELVE

LEXINGTON CHARLES

I could care less about being shot when I saw Averly run out of the car. When I saw Grecia running behind her, I didn't hesitate to put two bullets in his head. I have wanted to kill this nigga ever since I found out who he was. My father's men caught up to us at the gas station. I was shocked he stuck to his word.

I wrapped her tightly in my arms as I escorted her into the bulletproof truck. It didn't appear that Tonio and Grecia had any other gunmen out here with them. They were really stupid. They didn't think this out. I was relieved they didn't, or else I wouldn't have my wife back.

"I knew you would come for me, baby," she sobbed. Her shoulders bounced up and down as she poured out her heart to me.

"I'll never let you out of my sight again. I'm so sorry how things went down between us before you were kidnapped.

"I'm sorry too, baby. I gave you such a hard time."

"You wouldn't be you if you didn't," I smothered her with kisses.

The gunfire had stopped, and everything was finally quiet. Averly and I were inside the truck unbothered. Neither one of us was strangers to gunfire.

We had an army with us, so we weren't worried about anything. I was just glad to have this woman in my arms again.

"Baby girl," Juanita pulled open Averly's door with Neri behind her. Snatching her from my arms, she pulled her into hers. "Did they hurt you? What is Grecia doing here? Did you try and save you too?"

"Are you okay Averly Grace?" Her father interrupted.

"He was in on it. Tonio said he planted him. It was all a lie, Juanita. I'm okay, daddy. Thank you for coming for me."

"I will always come for you. You're my daughter," he beamed with adoration for her.

"Was getting you pregnant a part of it too?" She was genuinely confused.

"Potentially getting her pregnant," I corrected her. I knew now was not the time to worry about such a small matter, but I wasn't going to grind words.

Averly rubbed my hand and continued, "I was sick to my stomach when I found out what they did—playing with my life. I wish I had a gun; I would've blown their brains out myself.

"Well, Lexington did that for you," Juanita added.

"I want to see his body," she said.

Juanita and I looked at each other. "Are you sure?" I asked her.

"I'm sure, baby."

I helped her out of the truck. Her steps stuttered a bit once she was standing in front of Grecia's body.

Pffftt.

Averly spat in the center of his head, "Rest in hell, you snake," she kicked him. "Rest in heellllll," she collapsed, nearly hitting the ground had I not caught her.

"It's almost over, baby. We'll rain down hell on Tonio Rufino together. I promise I will make him suffer."

"I'm planning on it."

I got my wife back inside of the truck so that we could go home.

"Averly, there's something you should know," Neri started.

"Now is not the time Neri. I need to get my wife home safe and checked out by a doctor before you start dumping your garbage on her!"

"What's going on?" She raised from my chest.

"It's nothing. We can deal with it later," I assured her.

"Might as well do this now. We have a long drive ahead of us. Can't get any worse than me being kidnapped and having my baby's life threatened."

"As I said, this can wait."

"Lexington. I know you're trying to protect me, but it's okay."

"I'm a federal agent," Juanita blurted out.

"Juanita, I'm not in the mood for jokes. What do you both really have to tell me? Your sleeping together."

"Well, that too," Neri murmured.

Averly rolled her eyes, "I've known for years about you two."

"I really am an agent Averly," Juanita emphasized.

"How could you betray us like that? So this was all a lie? My whole life is a lie! The only thing real is my marriage! Did you even wait until my mother was buried before you mounted my father?"

They both were quiet as secret swirled around us like spirits of the dead looking in on the sins of the living.

"So you two were screwing around while my mother was alive? Did you two kill her too?"

"Your grandfather killed your mother, Averly," Juanita tried to explain.

"Stop lying!"

"It's true. He set her up with Dasante. He acted like he was interested in your mother. She fell in love with him. When she started an affair, he reported back to your grandfather. He had someone fill her tire way beyond the limit. She had a blowout on the highway, and well, you know the rest," Neri cosigned.

"Why didn't you save her?"

"I thought when she had you that he would let her live. Ten years later, he commenced the hit," Neri tried to provide as much clarity as he could.

"You coward. Both of you. Juanita, you probably wanted my mama out the way so you could play house! I hate both of you!"

"Averly Abarb was the one who tampered with your mother's car. I saw it on the-," Juanita attempted to plead her case.

"Don't! I just want silence the rest of the way home," she demanded.

They did as she asked. We decided it would be best if we stayed at the Saccone mansion until this is all resolved.

I ran Averly a bath in our old room. Well, the room I would go to when Averly pissed me off. I giggled, just thinking about how we would argue over the stupidest things.

I turned the jet streams on to help with Averly's sore muscles.

"Did they hurt you, my love?"

"No more than what Grecia normally did to me when I was dating him. He choked me out a few times. They fed me only enough to keep me alive, not that I had an appetite. I should've stayed long enough from them to draw my blood. You deserve to know if this baby is yours."

"I don't need a blood test to tell me I'm a father. I'm not in a rush for some test to validate me in our child's life. We know what it is, owner of my heart."

"Owner of your heart? You've been watching Vikings without me, haven't you?" Her eyes shot daggers.

"Woman, I haven't been posted in front of a T.V. while you're missing. Stop playing with me."

"I own your heart?"

"Always have and always will. I would paint this city red with blood to find you and our child. I will never let anyone hurt you again, Averly."

"Including my father and Juanita?"

Her countenance tumbled down into what I could tell was a dark place. She was torn by what she found out from those two.

Despite it all, I still believe Juanita loved Averly as her own daughter.

"Juanita loves you, and so does your dad. What they did was messed up, but no disrespect, it sounds like your mother had an equal part in how things played out. Your grandfather sounds like he was plotting to get her out of the family the entire time."

"That's what it sounds like. People who said our fathers killed her didn't know my grandfather was the puppet master behind the curtain. I can't believe he hated the color of her skin so much he would set her up. I can't believe she was stupid enough to fall for your dad of all people."

"Maybe she saw a part of him neither of us has. I've never seen anything in him worthy of love, but my mother and your mother did."

"You do love your father, Lexington."

"I'm loyal to my family. Yes, I spent years wanting his approval, but I don't love that hateful man Averly. It's too complicated to explain. Don't plague yourself with their mess. Take your time to process it in your own time. Tonight I'm taking in all of your beauty and essence I thought I would never see you again."

"I'll always come back to you, Lexington Charles. Not even death could keep me from you. I would haunt your dreams and fill your space with whatever is left of me."

I helped her into the tub. I watched as the bubbles covered her body. Beads of water danced on strands of her hair as her head rested on the white towel.

"I want to name our baby Alishia if it's a girl. That was the woman's name who helped me. I still have her phone. I need to get it back to her as soon as I can," she continued.

"Anything you desire owner of my heart."

"Make love to me, Lexington. Do it like it's the last time I would be on this earth."

"After you relax and unwind, I will do whatever you desire."

She flashed a lustful glance my way. If she weren't pregnant already, she would be after I was done with her tonight.

CHAPTER THIRTEEN

DASANTE CHARLES

Rimando Rufino did everything in his power not to sound anxious when he asked for a meeting with me. Their family has been slowly building strength in what little area the Bloody Five left for them in the city of Houston. He allowed the rejection of those clans to eat away at him for years. Years he attempted to weasel his way into the fold. He tried to get his son to marry Averly, but any blind man could see that girl wouldn't entertain someone so immature.

He's so hungry for the power it was no surprise at all his plan was botched. He has a brain capacity of a toddler.

My men told me about everything that went down at the farmhouse. The only thing I cared about was securing the seed growing inside of Averly Saccone. It was the key to me holding reign on the Bloody Five. It's now known as the Bloody Six since I joined.

I've been patiently moving pieces around like a chessboard. My ultimate goal is to be the last king standing.

"Mr. Charles. Mr. Rufino is waiting to speak with you," my servant notified me.

"You can send him in."

Rimando was a chubby man with dark black curly hair. The wine and pork from indulging in the pasta from his restaurant were seeping from his pores. I could see the sweat sitting on the outer layer of his skin.

"What can I do for you, Mr. Rufino? It's awful bold of you to show your face in my home after taking my daughter-in-law and unborn grandchild captive," I took another sip of my Hennessey.

"You know how idiotic Tonio can be at times. The boy is always trying to prove that he's ready to lead. I wanted to come and make it right."

"You wanted to come and ask something of me. What is it?"

"Join me," he leaned in closer, resting his elbows on my custom wood desk.

"Join you in what?"

"Taking Neri Saccone down! He sits in that ivory tower, looking down on the rest of us like he's some king! He's nothing of the sort! He ran his father's legacy in the ground."

"I'm not worried about Neri. I have that under control. I have an army behind me. Men who've been fighting for me for years that won't hesitate to die for my cause. What do you have to offer me?"

"More power. More men. We can attack and take what we want soon. You can sit at the head of the table. I just want the seat that I deserve," Rufino pleaded.

"What makes you think I'm not going to get that anyway?"

"The rest of the Bloody Five will never see you as one of them. Together we can wipe out that old blood and start anew. You do know that child she's carrying may not be your son's, right?"

"What?"

"They haven't told you?"

"Told me what?"

"Your daughter-in-law takes after her mother more than you realize. She slept with that ex of hers, Grecia, since she's been married to your son. When she disappeared for three days, she was at his home screwing his brains out."

"How do you know this?"

"Because I planted Grecia in her life years ago. You're not the only one who's been playing the long game, Dasante Charles. When I was robbing Neri's stash houses, I didn't expect him to get so desperate that he would come to you. I thought he would come to me to lift the pressure off of him."

"I was shocked myself, but we did bond back in the day. Neri had a knack for making poor decisions," I explained to Rimando.

"It appears he still does," Rimando co-signed.

"Well, when the plan is ready, then you let me know when and where. My men and I will be ready."

"Okay. It won't be long. The time to strike is now. An enemy took his daughter. He looks weak to the rest of the organization."

"That is true. There has been some murmuring amongst the other headships," I confirmed Rimando's allegations.

"Thank you for your time. I will be in contact soon," he stood and extended his arm. I looked at his hand and blew smoke instead from my cigar.

He needed me, so he ignored my disrespect and left. I can't believe Lexington didn't tell me that it could be another man's baby. He acted like that was the sole reason he was driven to protect her.

Has he truly fallen in love with his wife? If he has, then I need to lay him down with the rest. I refuse to look over my shoulder because I'm harboring a traitor. Son or not, he must die beside his wife.

I picked up the phone and pressed the number one button on my phone to dial the contact stored in the memory.

"Lexington has to go," was the order I gave before hanging up the phone.

CHAPTER FOURTEEN

AVERLY GRACE

Lexington and I quickly put some things into a suitcase. We were rushing to get to one of the safe houses.

"Dad, why are you standing here instead of packing?" I barked.

"This is the end of the line for him," Juanita spoke up.

"What do you mean?"

"He has to turn himself in. That's the only way to end all of this. If he testifies, then I may be able to work out a deal for him."

"Never snitch! Daddy, that's the foundation this family and organization were built on. How could you?"

"It's the only way to keep you and my grandchild safe. If I don't, one by one, the families in the Bloody Six will start to turn on us."

"You still have my father," Lexington assured my dad.

"Lexington, you know your father almost as well as I do. We both know he won't hesitate to betray any of us."

Lexington's lowered head gave the only confirmation we all needed. His father didn't care anything about him unless it was benefiting him.

"Averly, this is the only way to keep blood from spilling over into the streets. He's doing this for you."

"Y'all claim to do a lot for me, but none of you ever ask me what I want! You hide secrets from me and whisper in the wee hour's webs of deceit to tie me up in."

"Averly, I'm sorry I didn't save your mother. That I allowed my father to take her from you," my father drew in a long breath. A sorrowful expression flittered across his aging face.

"You were sleeping with Juanita. My mother would've been a fool not to seek love elsewhere. She made one mistake."

"It wasn't one mistake. Even after Elenor knew what Dasante did to her, she still kept sleeping with him. I wasn't sure you were mine, but I was relieved to find out you were. You've been a blessing since your first breath."

"When mom died, you were cold."

"It was guilt, Averly. Every time I looked at you, all I saw was your mother looking back at me. Reminding me of how I betrayed her."

"You've should've been stronger, daddy. It would help if you made better decisions. Now, look at this mess that was created! The Rufino's have been plotting because you rejected Rimando from the table based on a lie. You dishonored his family to hide what you and grandfather did. Now we're paying for it. All of us! Even your grandchild!"

"Can you ever forgive me, Averly Grace?"

"I will try. I can't think about that right now. I have to get my family to safety."

"I'm sending our best men with you," he insisted.

"That's not necessary. We don't know for sure if The Rufino's have gotten to them. My father also sent some of his best. They're waiting downstairs. We must go, love," Lexington interrupted us.

"Lexington Charles, please take care of my daughter. I don't know what will happen once I turn myself in, but you are a man of valor. I know you will keep her safe and protect her with your life."

"I promise I will," Lexington embraced my father. Physical contact was something I never saw him do with his father.

My father's pitiful eyes beckoned for me to do the same.

I slowly walked up to him and allowed him to embrace me. "I will love you forever, my daughter."

"I love you too, daddy. Always and forever."

CHAPTER FIFTEEN

JUANITA ALVAREZ

Pain funneled into my heart as we drove to the bureau. Neri was focused on nothing in particular, on the outside of the window.

"Do you regret it?" I asked Neri.

"Regret what?"

"Hiring me."

"Not at all."

"Really?"

"Really, Juanita. Had I not hired you, they would've planted someone else. Who knows how things would've gone after I asked them to help discard the first body? It was hard for me to believe because of the things you helped me do."

The tires screeched as the truck careened to a stop on the side of the road, "The only thing I regret is being an agent now. I know you probably don't believe me, but I love you and Averly Grace down to my bones."

"I know you do. I know this is hard for you, but I'd be lying if I didn't say your betrayal didn't hurt," Neri said, his voice was sweet and smooth like syrup. "I'm afraid for my daughter," his forehead creased with worry. "Promise me that no matter what, you will look after her. She's mad right now, but you know you're the only mother she knows."

"I love Averly like my own daughter. You know that! I will guard her with my life." A relieved look washed across his face. "The only reason I'm not by her side is that I have to make sure I secure your immunity. I'm retiring after this case. This has all been too stressful."

"Is everything okay?" His eyebrows formed a hairy M in the center of his head.

"I'm fine. I never expected to fall in love with you, Neri Saccone. This assignment hasn't been easy. I fed them just enough to keep them on the case, but they don't know about any of the bodies. The laundering, construction schemes, and drugs are what they are aware of. Even with that, I implicated the other family heads like the ones pulling strings. I had to paint you as being washed up and over your head so they will think you only can offer information. I tried to work it where you can get immunity."

"Were you able to?" He asked.

"Depends on what you tell them."

A flash of movement caught my eye, "Get down!" I screamed, throwing my body over his. I had my vest on, but depending on what they were using, it may not be of any use.

Tak!

Tak!

Tak!

I pulled my Glock out and blasted back from my window while jamming the car into gear. I blindly pulled the vehicle from the side of the road. I floored the gas, trying to get us out of that jam.

"Are you okay?" I frantically patted his body down with my free hand.

"It's just a flesh wound," he rubbed his face with both hands. When he dropped his hands back down on his knees with a slap, his hair was sticking up where he had ruffled it, and his eyes looked wide, if not a little manic.

My eyes bulged as wide as two hot pies cooling in a window seal, "Oh God, you've been hit!"

"I've had worse. Who knew you were bringing me in?"

"It's a team of us, but we don't have any moles."

"We didn't tell anyone else!"

"Do you think Lexington told his dad?"

"I don't think so. Even with Averly being missing, he chose to stay at the house with me," he pulled up his button-up and ripped a piece of his undershirt to wrap around his arm.

"Let me get you to the hospital."

"No, if any of the other families know what's about to happen, we need to get there now!"

"Okay."

"You know I will never stop loving you, Juanita. It's quite ironic that I fell in love with an agent if you think about it," he chuckled.

I was constantly watching my rearview to make sure we weren't being followed. The back of my Charger scraped the cement as I sped into the under-car garage.

"Why didn't you just pull in the front. Anyone could be down here ready to shoot us," paranoia swallowed the color in Neri's skin.

"We're safe here," I unbuttoned my shirt.

"What are you doing?"

"I don't know how this is going to end, but I'm sure a quickie for old times' sake couldn't hurt."

"You're right about that," he flashed a crooked grin.

We both hungrily ripped away our clothes. Neither of us knew what the future held, but we were about to make our last moments count.

Nothing like a good shoot-out to get you in the mood for some goodbye sex.

*   *   *

After a thorough forty minutes of pleasure, I walked Neri Saccone into the station. As a formality, I had my cuffs on him. I couldn't help but think how much fun it could be now that he knows who I really am.

A huge weight had lifted off me when I told him and Averly Grace.

"Great job Alvarez," my counterpart congratulated me as I walked in with Neri.

They were proud, but I was breaking inside with every step I took to the interrogation room. Neri's face was void of all emotion. The vulnerable man in the car had disappeared, leaving Neri "Trigger Finger" Saccone.

"Alvarez, you can watch from the other side. If we need you, we will call you in," my captain assured me.

"But this is my case!"

"It's still your case, but we need to see what he has to say without you in the room."

He didn't wait for an answer before disappearing into the room with Neri.

I hurried to the room to listen in with a few other agents working the case on the other families.

"Before we do anything, I want my lawyer here. If I'm going to be a rat, I need certain conditions met."

"We have enough on you alone to put you under the federal prison!"

"Why settle for me when I'm willing to hand you the Bloody Five on a silver platter?"

My captain was cemented in place by Neri's question. We've been chasing the Bloody Five for years but could never nail anyone but the foot soldiers. To get them under the Rico Act, we need to tie them all together. Aren't you the Bloody Six now, though?"

"Yeah, but I don't know much about them. The Mamba Mafia just joined us recently."

"I'm sure there's something you can give us."

"As soon as my lawyer gets here."

"Fine." He looked up at the double-sided mirror and said, "Juanita, bring him his phone."

I reached into the plastic bag marked "evidence" and took it into the room. Neri's eyes met mine but the love no longer poured from them.

This was the Neri I witnessed slice someone's throat down to the bone for stealing for him. The cold Neri.

I exited the room and went back to being a spectator.

Neri scrolled through his contacts and called all three of his lawyers.

"Would you like anything while we wait?" My captain offered.

"You're not getting my DNA without the proper chain of command. I'm good."

My captain leaned back in his chair in admiration, "I see this is not your first rodeo."

"No. It's not."

Neri's lawyers arrived within twenty minutes suited, booted, and ready for war.

"We need the District Attorney to come from behind that glass and into this room," the tall Caucasian one with a tailored suit demanded.

"And tell her to bring her pencil pusher," the African American one that was only about five feet with his shoes on added.

The other one looked like a white hippie sat there quietly with a smirk on his face.

"Guess I have to earn my pay today," Georgia sighed.

She was a shapely African American woman with a non-existent waist and full butt and hips, and elegantly styled locs. Her suit was tailored as well. I knew because she bragged about it often. Love it or hate, every case she tried, she got a conviction. I was glad to see her. She was notorious for using the smaller fish to catch the larger ones. I prayed she saw Neri as just that.

She sauntered into the room, "Ask, and you shall receive."

"My client has beneficial information for you. We need this to be beneficial for him as well," the short lawyer spoke up.

"What are you asking?"

"Immunity as long as he testifies. Protection before and after the trial."

"Just before. After I'm disappearing," Neri interrupted.

"Give me something that will make my toes spread," Georgia sat her round backside on the desk next to my man. My blood started to boil under my skin.

She crossed one thigh over the other. Neri's eyes scanned the length of both. He's always had a thing for chocolate women. They were and always be his weakness.

"I can give you the other five on a silver platter. I can give you recordings, bodies, and records. Do you want to know how many of your cops are on our payroll? We are embedded into everything in this city that's lucrative."

"Okay. I'll bite Mr. Saccone. Give me what I need to end up on Good Morning America, and you can have your immunity. Testify, and I could care less where you go after. Draw up the paperwork," she spat to her pen pusher. "If you don't testify, this will all go away. I will make you wish you were never born if you betray me, Mr. Saccone," she threatened him.

CHAPTER SIXTEEN

LEXINGTON CHARLES

The polished marble flooring gleamed in the full sun as our guards ushered us in. I knew Neri didn't ask for specific details because we all just found out Juanita was a FED. He had no guarantees of how this would go, and he didn't want us in the crosshairs of what was about to go down.

"Take our bags up to the bedroom," I ordered a couple of them.

Averly didn't say a word as she made her way to the seamless windows and breathtaking view of the horses running wild on the property. My father bought the property on the outskirts of Lufkin, Texas, several years ago. It was gated, quiet, and immaculate even for property in the country.

I towered over her from behind as I placed kisses on her neck, "Are you okay?"

I was concerned about her. She was kidnapped, her life hung in the balance, she found out the mother that raised her was a Fed, and her father just turned himself in to save our family.

That was too much for anyone to bear. Averly and her father's relationship was strained, but they were all they had over the years after her mother's untimely death. A death my father and hers had hands in.

"I don't know," she uttered.

"Your father is on his way here?" The guard advised me.

"Why?"

"He said you could call him if you'd like," he shrugged.

"Baby, I'm going to call and make sure everything is okay. Do you need anything?"

"No, I love it here. We should move to someplace like this to raise the baby," she smiled from ear to ear.

"Anything you want," I kissed her forehead before walking away to call my dad.

I waited as the phone rang a couple of times. He finally picked up, "Dad, they said you're on your way here. Wassup?"

"It's a lot going on. I just want to be there with you both. Is Neri on his way?"

"No, he had some business he said he had to take care of."

"Oh, make sure he comes. We should all be at the safe house until we figure this out."

"Okay, I will check upon him," I lied.

There ain't no way I was about to tell my daddy this man turned himself in. This nigga barely liked me. If he found out Neri was snitching, he would use it as an opportunity to take over the Bloody Six. He wouldn't hesitate to have my wife and me killed. I hung up the phone and returned to Averly Grace.

"My daddy on his way here."

"Why?"

"With everything that's happening, he said he feels better if he was here with us. He asked, was Neri on his way?"

"What did you tell him?"

"He had some business to take care of, but I will check in on him."

"Thank God."

"I already know, babe. I don't trust him either."

"I hate you're in this predicament."

"Our father's put us in this predicament. We've turned it into something solid, but the fight is just beginning. When you're father hands the organization over on a silver platter, they will want blood. Your father made some mistakes, but he loves you. My father has only glorified being a part of the Bloody Five and being on top. If he had to kill me to get there, he would."

"So, what are we going to do when he gets here?"

"Stay on point. I don't know where Dasante's head is at because I haven't been talking to him. I didn't put pressure on him to help me find you until I started getting scared that I never would."

"For real?"

"Girl, you collapsed my lungs when you went missing. We were beefing about the baby, we made up, and the next thing I know, you didn't come home. I can handle anything but trying to live without you by my side. We were forced into this, but it looks like this was one thing our parents got right. You're my world, Averly Grace."

"Are you happy at me?"

"What?" I laughed.

"Are you happy at me?"

"I'm happy at you, baby," I kissed her lips.

"Oh," she broke away.

"What's wrong?"

"The baby. It kicked," she placed her hand on her protruding stomach.

"Can I feel?"

"Yeah, babe."

Sure enough, I put my hand on her stomach, and the baby kicked.

"I can't wait to become a dad Averly Grace. Thank you for this gift. I hope it's a girl that looks just like you."

"You don't want a boy?"

"Not yet. I know he's going to be hard-headed like me."

"She's probably going to have my smart mouth if it is a girl."

"I'm sure she will. Babe, can you go to the back before my dad gets here?"

"Why are you trying to hide me like some secret in the back room?"

"It's not that. We have a lot going on. If things go left, I don't want you or the baby in harm's way. That's all."

"I can handle myself," the click-clack of her gun caught my attention. "I'm still getting my bearings, but I'm sure a little target practice will whip me right into shape."

"Babe, please don't give me a hard time about this. Go unpack and get settled in. I'll bring you something to eat as soon as I find out what my dad is really coming here for."

"You think he knows about my dad?"

"I don't know. How could he? My dad has people everywhere. I'm not sure what he knows, which is why I want you out of the way!"

"Are you really prepared to kill your dad?"

"If that's what it takes to save you and our child, absolutely. I'm not going to let anyone hurt you."

"I'm not about to have you face him without me having your back either!"

"Averly, just take your butt to the back! I don't have time for this back and forth!"

Without uttering another word, she stomped down the hallway to our bedroom and slammed the door.

I just shook my head. I'll make it up to her later. Right now, I needed to be prepared for anything. My father was devious. He would smile in my face while pulling the trigger to blow my wife's brains out.

I stood on the front cobblestone steps as my father's Ford F450 made its way down the red dirt road. He was driving so fast a small cloud of red dust seemed like it was chasing the truck.

I waited until he had parked the truck. He, along with a few of his guards, hopped out.

"Did they have everything set up when you got here? I sent the cleaning crew out as soon as you told me you were headed out there."

"Yes, they had everything cleaned and stocked."

"Is Neri here yet?"

"He's not going to be able to make it here," I informed him.

"No, you're not hearing me. You need to get Neri here now! I mean right now!"

"What's going on?" I walked back inside, freeing the snap on my holster around my gun.

"I'm tired of playing nice. Even with you marrying that girl, they still treat us like second-class citizens. They still call it the Bloody Five even though our family made it six. My organization has been stronger than Neri's. I can take what I want!" He brandished his Beretta before pointing it at me.

"So you're going to shoot me? Your only surviving son."

"Without thinking twice! You're not my only surviving son. You know what I've sacrificed and gave up to get here. I'm not going to let what Neri has going on stop me when I'm this close to taking it all over!"

I hesitated, reaching for my pistol because I knew he would let his rip. If that happened, my father would kill Averly as soon as she had our baby.

He took three ground eating steps, "Step to the side! I bet he comes for that slut you're ready to die protecting."

"Don't disrespect my wife!" I pulled my pistol out and pointed it back at him.

"You have fallen in love with her?"

My father made a tsk-ing noise with his mouth.

"We've fallen in love with each other," I retorted.

"Is that so? Sure about that son?"

"What's taking so long?" Tonio walked into the house like he paid the mortgage.

"What is this nigga doing here?"

"I'm not a nig-"

My father's death stare severed the rest of his sentence before he could finish.

"Go find out where he has her!" My father instructed Tonio.

"Don't let him anywhere near my wife!" I commanded my guards, but they just stood there. "Don't y'all hear me talking?"

"They take their orders from me. Why do you think I made sure only our men were here with you? You aren't as smart as you think, Lexington," he scoffed.

"After the way he treated y'all? I made sure to put money in your pockets so you could get a piece of the pie for yourselves, and this is how you repay me?"

"Loyalty bought with money can waver, son. I taught you that long ago."

I shrank in defeat, trying to figure out a way to get Averly and me out of this jam. I was regretting not allowing her to stay as she insisted. At least I knew she had my back for sure.

"If you touch my wife, I will kill you!" I threatened Tonio as he rushed down the corridor towards the bedroom.

"Why am I not hearing any killing," Rimando Rufino walked in the opened door to join the fiasco.

"He's not here," my father told him.

"What the-" I heard Averly scream.

Pop!

Pop!

"Averly!" I spun around so fast I nearly fell. If my dad wanted to shoot me, he could.

My father's henchman tackled me as I crawled on my hands and knees, trying to get to my wife.

"I will bury all of you if anything has happened to her!" I screamed as tears stung my eyes. "Averly, baby, say something!"

Averly appeared from the corridor with a gun in each hand. "I told you that you needed me up here to have your back," she smirked.

"If you hurt my son-"

"I killed your son!" She spat.

"I will cut that baby out of you myself," Rimando pulled out his butterfly knife with his free hand.

"Try it. You fat butterball turkey!"

"Drop your guns, Averly Grace, or I will blow his brains out in front of you," my father pressed his gun in the back of my head.

"Don't do it, babe!" I grunted as I squirmed to get free.

"I'm not going to let anyone hurt you, Lexington," her voice stuttered.

She bent at the waist, laying her guns on the marble floor. "If you're going to shoot me, then go ahead. I'm not about to beg for my life like a coward."

"Baby chill," I coached her.

My father would put a bullet in her head without thinking twice.

Her weight shifted back and forth as she rocked from side to side. Her eyes were bucked, watching every movement in the room. Despite our lives hanging in the balance, her breathing was steady.

This wasn't our first shoot-out, but it may be our last if Rimando and my dad had their way.

"Loving you has been my greatest joy, Lexington Charles. I'm proud to be your wife. You're nothing like him," her eyes raised to my father. "You're better than him. Always was. That's why he tried to crush you under his jealousy."

"Don't pretend to know anything about my son and me; you washed up slut! You just like yo' mama!"

"Don't speak on her, you coward! You were so desperate to be a part of something that never wanted you that you sacrificed her!"

"I'm going to enjoy killing you and that bastard in your stomach!" My father moved closer.

"Watch ya' mouth!" I struggled to get away from my dad's henchman.

"I'm not afraid, Lexington. I love you!" Averly refused to let a tear fall despite looking down the barrel of my father's gun.

"I'll love you even in the afterlife, baby. I'll see you on the other side. I won't even let death separate us. You deserved so much better than this. I tried to stop your heart from bleeding out."

"You did," she smiled, in the face of the danger, we were suffocated by.

Kssshh!

Kssshh!

Kssshh!

Three smoke grenades were launched through the windows startling all of us.

"Averly!" I freed myself from the guards and swooped my wife into my arms.

Tak!

Tak!

Tak!

Pop!

Pop!

Tak!

With all the commotion going on, I was able to drag Averly by her wrist. We both still had our guns in hand.

"Aaahhh!" Averly's high-pitched scream stopped me dead in my tracks.

She faltered against the wall staining it with her blood. It poured out so liberally I couldn't tell where it was coming from.

"You've been shot!" I panicked.

Pop!

Out of the corner of my eye, I noticed Rimando put a bullet in the back of my father's head. He should've known he couldn't trust the Rufino's, but his thirst for power consumed him.

"Hold on, baby," I carried her down the dim tunnel that led us off the property.

"Let me get the keys," I huffed, gently placing her on the soft patch of grass.

I felt around the front tire until I found the magnetic key holder. I opened it and removed the spare key. I started the car before placing Averly in the passenger seat.

"Averly stay with me!" I yelled, watching her eyes rolled to the back of her head.

CHAPTER SEVENTEEN

LEXINGTON CHARLES

We swerved to the right as the car's back end fishtailed until it came to a halt. The driver's door gave up a squeaky yawn before spitting me on my feet.

"I need help!" I howled, carrying my unconscious blood-stained wife in my arm. "She's been shot!"

The nurses and a doctor sprinted towards me. One of them wheeled a bed out to put her on. I watched as they got her vitals. Another nurse wheeled a metal IV stand with saline next to her.

A thin curtain was the only thing giving her any bit of privacy. I heard them page the OB/GYN to the ER stat. The beep of the heart monitor let me know my wife was still fighting.

The smell of latex gloves and over-bleached sheets stung my nose. Averly squinted at the bright light the doctor shoved in her face when he peeled one of her eyelids up.

"She pregnant! Please save them," I pleaded.

"Stay here, please," one of the nurses demanded, sitting me in the hallway. "I'll be out to get you personally once we've stabilized her. We need to get some information. Take a seat so our registration clerk can get her into the system."

"Okay."

I was a zombie while I handed her our insurance cards and gave her all of the necessary information to help Averly.

"Is there someone I can call to be here with you?" She asked.

"No, I can handle it."

"Take a seat in the waiting room. A police officer will be here to speak with you in just a moment. One of the nurses will be out to get you as soon as they can."

"Okay."

I walked over to a corner near the double emergency doors but far enough away to have a private conversation.

My hands were sticky from Averly's blood that had started to dry. I rang them together as I prayed for God to intervene and save my wife and child.

The phone rang and rang, but Juanita didn't pick up. That was the only person I had to call. The only person other than Neri that cared about Averly as much as I did.

As soon as I sat my phone down, it started to vibrate. Juanita's number flashing across my phone screen gave me some relief.

"Hello."

"Are you both okay? I searched for you but didn't see you at the safe house. Averly texted me the address when you both arrived. Neri gave us enough to take down Tonio, Rimando, and several other Bloody Six leaders. How is Averly?"

I could hear a lot of commotion in the background. I wanted to ask her if my father was dead, but there was no way he survived being shot in the head.

Groanings filled my throat, "She was shot."

"Oh, my God! I'll be there as soon as I can. Is she okay?"

"I don't know. The doctors won't let me back to see her yet. I can't lose her again, Juanita. She's all that I have left."

"I'm sorry about your father. I know he wasn't the best to you, but he was still your dad."

My chest tightened with guilt. My father was a plague in my life, but Juanita was right. He was still my father.

"Thank you. You, Neri, and Averly are my family now."

"I know it doesn't seem like it, but I promise you everything will be okay," Juanita assured me.

"I hope so. My only concern right now is my wife and child."

"I understand. I will be there soon. I will let Averly's father know what is going on as well."

"Juanita, they said a cop would be here to speak with me soon. How much do they know?"

"Just tell them your parent's dealings put you both in harm's way. You were taken to a safe house where you were attacked. Everything after that is a blur."

"I understand."

"Be there as soon as I can. I promise," she ended the call abruptly.

I sat in the corner, replaying my father take a bullet to the head.

"I'm sorry, dad," I muttered tearfully to myself before taking a deep breath—a bucketful of thoughts needed to go, to make room for the new ones.

"Mr. Charles," the nurse who gave me her word called to me.

I jogged over to meet her, "How is my wife?"

"She going into surgery. I'm not going to lie. It's not looking good for either of them, but we have the best surgeons on staff here. They're flying in a specialist for the baby as well. Once she's out of surgery, we will let you come back and sit with her and your daughter until she's moved to her room."

"Daughter?"

"Oh, I'm sorry. Did you guys not want to know?"

"We've just had so much going on we haven't had the chance to find out."

"Well, congratulations. I'll be back when I find out more."

*   *   *

After eight grueling hours, the nurse reappeared, "I'm sorry it's taken so long. She has been moved to her room. The doctor felt it would be best to make sure she was out of recovery before coming to get you.

"Are they okay?"

"You have a couple of fighters. They both pulled through like rock stars," she thrust her fist in the sky.

Warmth radiated through my body at the sound of her words.

She escorted me to the elevators. I took one up to the fourth floor.

We walked past several rooms before arriving at my wife's.

"When will she wake up?"

"The sedation is still wearing off. It will be hard to tell."

"Is she in any pain?"

"They have her on something for the pain."

"Is it safe for the baby?"

"Yes, she's a bit high with mom, but she's going to be okay."

"Will she-"

"Mr. Charles, they are out of the woods. It's a waiting game now."

I drug the outdated metal chair positioned next to her bed closer to hold her hand.

"Can I bring you anything?"

"No, thank you."

"We also made sure to keep her unlisted as you requested."

"Thank you."

Once she was out of the room, I text Juanita the information so she would be able to find us. She's an agent, so I'm sure she would've been able to get in without my help.

My shaking leg made the water from my eyes fall. I searched within myself for resolutions to help my wife and daughter.

Averly is going to be so excited to find out she's having a mini her.

"You're having a girl Averly Grace Charles," I muttered, planting soft kisses on her cheek.

I called my florist to have them deliver her favorite flower, the Bleeding Heart. I paid to have them construct a greenhouse specifically to grow them for her while I had the one built at home. I got tired of trying to get them transported in.

Averly's voice struck upward as she struggled to adjust the tubes.

"No, baby, you can't take those out," I gently removed her hands before she snatched the wrong thing out. "They are still monitoring both of you."

She moaned out in agony. I pressed the red button to call for her the nurse, "Can someone please come and check on my wife?"

"We'll be right in."

They rushed into the room with the doctor, "Her vitals are strong. So is the baby's," the doctor nodded at me, removing his stethoscope from his ears.

"We're going to take her up for a couple of tests."

"Okay."

"You can wait here for her," he rested his hand on my chest.

I kissed Averly, "They're going to take you for another test, baby. I'll be waiting right here when you get back. I promise.

Her eyes pleaded for me to go with her because she was afraid.

"It's going to be okay. I promise."

I watched them unhook some of the wires so they could wheel her out of the room. Once she was down the hall, I broke down.

I was just grateful to the Most High that my family was okay. All of the prayers I stored up were paying off. I clutched my chest as my tears soaked my unbuttoned shirt. My tongue felt fuzzy. I couldn't remember the last time I'd brushed my teeth. Hygiene was the last thing on my mind while the life of my wife and child hung in the balance.

"Is everything okay?" I quickly attempted to dry my face as Juanita entered the room.

"Yes, everything is fine. They just took Averly for a couple more tests," I wiped my eyes with the back of my hand.

"How is Neri?"

"He's fine. They have him in protective custody for now until we round up everyone on the indictment."

"I guess congratulations are in order."

"No, I'm retiring. This has been the longest case of my life. I'm tired. I just want this to be done. How are you holding up?"

"You mean despite my mini-breakdown? I'm okay. Averly and I have grown so much since this all first started. At one point, we couldn't stand the sight of one another, and now our bodies ache when we're apart."

"Yes, I'm familiar with that type of love."

"Are the Feds coming after Averly and me?"

"No, you both are in the clear. I assured them you were ignorant of both your father's illegal actions."

"They believed you?"

"I hope so. As far as I know, they aren't looking into either of you. Neri's attorney's made sure you both were included in his immunity deal anyway."

"Really?"

"Yes. I'm not saying Neri doesn't have his ways. His father despised him because he felt like Neri was soft. Luca felt the way Neri loved those around him made him vulnerable. He thought revealing who Elenor was to him would break him, but it didn't. It just made him cling to me even more after she was killed. I'm not proud of how things started between us, but it is what it is. We can only make the best of it and move forward. Why don't you go home and clean up while she's getting her tests? I won't leave her side until you return."

"Thank you, but no thanks. I'll run down to the cafeteria to get some coffee, but I'm not leaving her vulnerable again."

Juanita's smile stretched from ear to ear, "Well, I will sit here until you come back from the cafeteria then."

"Thank you."

CHAPTER EIGHTEEN

JUANITA ALVAREZ

Lexington rolled his body out of the chair like he was lifting a sack of bricks.

"You okay? Did they check you out?"

"No, but I assured them I was fine," Lexington grumbled.

"Are you?"

"I'm good," he rubbed both eyes with the butt of his hands. "I won't be gone long."

"Take your time."

Hours had gone by, and still no word from Lexington. I wasn't sure if he had taken me up on my offer for him to go home and clean up or not, but he'd been gone for quite some time. I didn't mind. My throat was starting to tighten when I thought about what I should say to Averly.

How do you explain to a woman you raised as your daughter why you betrayed her and her father? The two people you loved more than anything in this world.

I was so dedicated to her and Neri that I never bothered to have kids of my own. If Neri wasn't the father, I didn't want any parts to create a life without him.

I hurried to my feet when I saw them wheeling Averly Grace back into her room. Surprisingly, she welcomed me with a smile. I could tell it was taking an effort for her, but she did it.

"How are you, *mi amour*?"

"I've been better. That's for sure."

"I just wanted to say-"

"You don't have to explain, Juanita."

"But I do. I'm sorry for betraying you both. When I took the job, I had no idea I would fall in love with you and your father."

"I know you love me, Juanita. No one can tell me you faked that. You held me many nights and wiped my tears as I cried myself to sleep. You even came to pick me up when Lexington left me in a hotel room years ago. Funny how things change," she moaned in agony.

"Yes, it is," my breath fell out softly from my lips.

"I want you to be the baby's Godmother. Will you?"

"How can I say no to something so amazing. Of course, I will. I will love her just as much as I love you, maybe more."

"Thank you. I know you will. How is my father?"

"He's in protective custody. Of course, the Bloody Six has animosity. We took down the leaders, but we don't know for sure who's all in the wind. We're not ignorant to the fact that they can still order hits. You'll have a few guards to keep you and Lexington safe as well."

"I assumed as much. Do you think the trial will happen after I have the baby?"

"Yes, it's going to take them a while to get everything for the trial. The U.S. District Attorney on the case, Georgia Woods, doesn't play. She's very thorough, and she's never lost a case."

"All the more reason I need to be by my father's side as he goes through this."

"What?"

"A lot has come to light to explain my father's actions over the years. I want to be there for him as our family goes through this. I want him to come home and spoil his grandbaby. Can you keep everything together until I deliver?"

"You know I can. Whatever you need me to do, just let me know! I know we dumped a lot on you. I should've come clean earlier, but I was afraid I would lose you."

"You're all I have. I know firsthand that things are more complicated than we would like them to be. I'm praying this baby belongs to my husband. I know Lexington will love it regardless, but I just don't' want any part of Grecia now that I know it was all a lie."

"I can understand that. I also know that you will love your baby fiercely despite who the father is. You're going to be a great mother."

"I hope so."

"You will be."

"I'm sorry I took so long," Lexington walked into the room. "My phone has been blowing up since the death of my father.

"What?" Averly tried to rest on her elbows, but the pain caused her to collapse back on the bed.

"Don't try to sit up yet," Lexington scolded her.

"He's dead? How?"

"A bullet to the head by Rimando Rufino," he pulled his chair closer to her bedside.

"Are you okay, babe?"

"He was trying to betray us. All the guards there were working for him. I knew who my father was, but I would be lying if I said that I wasn't hurting. I'm not worried about that right now. You're my only concern."

"Why are they calling you after they help your dad set us up."

"They follow the orders of whoever is in charge. Averly, I'm not about to talk about that. That's the least of my worries."

Watching Averly somewhat comply with what her husband said let me know she really did love him. She was like a dog with a bone when she wanted to know something.

"I asked Juanita to be the baby's Godmother," she gently squeezed his hand.

He looked at his wife and then at me. His eyes lowered to meet hers, "I think that's a great idea."

"Really?"

"Yes, despite what we're going through, Juanita has still been loyal. I need that kind of love around my daughter."

"Daughter," she looked up at Lexington.

"Yes, they did an ultrasound when you came in the E.R. It's a girl."

"I could feel it was a girl. If Juanita kept me safe, I know Alisha will be in good hands."

"That's her name?" I asked Averly Grace."

"Yes, that's the name of the nurse that helped me at the clinic."

"Well, isn't that sweet," Georgia Woods, the U.S. District Attorney, interrupted our conversation. "Agent Alvarez, don't you think it's inappropriate for you to be here?"

"No, it's not," I replied flatly.

"Ms. Saccone, I-"

"It's Mrs. Charles, and what can I do for you?"

"I just wanted to come and make sure you were okay. I heard about the shootout."

"Thank you. As you see, this is a moment I'm sharing with family."

Sarcasm filled the pockets of the air. Averly and Georgia's interaction was cringy.

"District Attorney, may I speak to you outside?"

I had to get her out of Averly's face before this all went left. I wanted to know why she was here.

"Yes, I have to be going anyway. Here is my card Averly," she extended her hand, but Averly just mugged her.

"I'll take it. As my wife said, we are celebrating the life of my child and me. Thank you so much for stopping by, though."

Georgia shoved her mouth to one side, accenting her high cheekbones with her devious smirk.

"You're welcome. I'll be in touch."

I took short, fast-paced steps back and forth across a total of four-floor tiles as I waited for Georgia in the hallway.

"What was that about?"

"What do you mean?"

"We may still need her and him down the line in this trial. I have to use the leverage I've gained in their family and lives."

She stood there doing her best to read me. I don't care how good an attorney she was; this is what they trained me for in the bureau.

"I didn't know you were still on the case since we have Neri handing the Bloody Six over to us on a silver platter."

"I'm working this case until we have as many of them are behind bars as possible!"

"I got you. Here is my cell phone number," she handed me a card similar to the one she gave Lexington.

I quickly shoved it into my pocket.

I let out the oxygen I stuffed inside my chest until Georgia was out of sight.

"So, you just playing us all, huh?" Lexington startled me. "You let my wife sit there and make you the God Mother of our child while you sit out here in the hallway getting in cahoots with the U.S. District Attorney.!"

"I promise you that's not the case."

"Well, I guess we won't know for sure until this is all over. You could be working on a case on me for all I know since my father is dead."

"I can explain, Lexington."

"Don't bother. You've been bumping your gums enough, don't you think?"

Before I could answer him, he stormed out of the hallway back inside Averly's room. He slammed the door, but you really couldn't tell because it was heavier than it appeared.

The more I tried to make things better; it seemed like I was only making matters worse.

I didn't want Averly to pick up on the tension between her husband and me, so I decided to leave. Lexington was right. There would be no way to prove whose side I'm on until this was all over. As much as I loved them all, it still wasn't an easy decision to burn my career that I've built to the ground. This is a career-making bust, and the recognition was already starting to roll in.

The Commissioner personally sat down with me to express his gratitude before I came to check on Averly.

The city has been after the Bloody Five for years. When they added Dasante Charles' clan, the bureau started applying more pressure to get the case closed.

I stopped at the nearby Chinese Restaurant for an order of shrimp fried rice and Egg Foo Yung in brown gravy.

My tires moaned as I put the car in park. Emptiness poured into me as I looked up at my bedroom window.

It may seem delusional, but cooking, cleaning, caring for Neri, Averly, and Lexington made me feel like I was the doting wife and mother.

My reality waited to slice me from ear to ear like a predator awaiting its prey. I grabbed my food and case files as I headed inside.

I studied my surroundings, making sure no one was lying in wait for me. They shouldn't find me here, but you never know the full reach of the mafia until it's too late.

Clumsily I climbed the stairs from memory with my hands filled in a desperate attempt not to make multiple trips to the car. My takeout dangled between my crooked teeth.

I could feel some of my manilla files slipping. I levered my weight against the front door as I maneuvered the key into the lock.

I dropped everything on the living room table so I could sort through it. I grabbed the bag of food from my mouth before I fell and decorated my paperwork with soy sauce-drenched rice and brown gravy.

Images of Neri danced in my head, making it nearly impossible to fight the feeling of going to his mansion and crawling into his bed. When this is all done, how would it even be possible to have a life with Neri? Maybe I was just delusional about all of this. I need to ponder closing my heart when I complete this case. It may be the best move for all of us.

CHAPTER NINETEEN

AVERLY GRACE

Six months later...

"Averly, you need to calm down! If anyone of them gets outside of their body, I'm going to jail. You need just to chill out!"

"Nah, they not about to keep treating me like I'm a prisoner! We both know we can handle ourselves!"

Lexington was scolding me yet again like I was some sort of child! This baby has taken over my body, and I'm stressed out about this trial.

"That's not the point, Averly. You agreed not to make this difficult."

"There's a difference between having guards and being treated like we're in witness protection already," I huffed, folding my arms across my full breast.

The baby had me gaining weight in all the right places. We couldn't keep our hands off each other. Well, when I'm not firing these agents up.

"I'll talk to Juanita so we can see if we can hire our own security detail. That way you can have more freedom. Babe, you have to understand that I'm not trying to lose you either. You know I hate telling you no, but this is for your good."

"I know, but if you can make it happen with our security team, that would be perfect. I won't get on your nerves again for another one to two business days," I leaned into his bulging chest. "Oh, and don't forget you have to go to that doctor's office those jerks took me to. They need to test you, for you know," I lowered my head in shame.

I decided to finish up the testing there. I know it's weird, but despite being kidnapped. I liked the atmosphere. I was bummed when I found out Alishia wasn't working the day I came. So, hopefully, she's there when we go for the results.

"Stop lowering your head every time you have to bring up the paternity of our daughter Averly. You were forced into an impossible predicament. You handled it the best way you could at that moment. We're not in that place anymore. We're here; in the future, we're carving out one bullet at a time. I'd do anything for you," he promised.

"You're making a woman out of me, Mr. Lexington Charles. How have you been with, ya know?"

"Averly, you can say my dad died."

"I know. It's still just weird. You cremated him and kind of just went about your day. Lexington, you still haven't picked up his ashes from the funeral home yet. Those people keep calling us to come to get your daddy."

"I have a lot of emotions I'm still working through. That man was my hero. I hung on his every word like it was the Bible or something Averly. To mistreat me is one thing, but to think I would allow him to hurt you was it for me."

"Listen, baby," I pulled him by his jewelry cluttered wrist. "What our fathers did is on them, not us. We have a baby coming. That's all that matters now. She is our future. What they did is our past. I know you love your father. There's nothing wrong with that. You need to put him in the past where he belongs. It sounds callous, but I chose you. I'm not about to let this man bury you even in death. Be at peace knowing that you survived that man despite how he attempted to obliterate you."

"I want to renew our vows," he quickly changed the subject, pushing away my speech from his mind.

"Not while I'm fat like this," I whined.

"No, you left me hanging on our wedding day, so this one will be on my terms. It's my turn to have the wedding of my dreams with this good thing I have found," he nuzzled into the length of my neck.

"Oh, Lord. So what are we having? Hot wings and forties," I chuckled.

"Cut it out. You know I don't get down like that. It's going to be classier than that funeral you coordinated for our wedding."

"I know you didn't. My décor didn't look like no dog on funeral!"

"Don't make me pull up evidence."

"Please do!"

I watched him pull his phone out of his tight slacks.

"You love dressing like a whore don't you?"

"What are you talking about, woman? Geez, Louise!"

"Them pants so tight you can't even get your phone out. You like them ole' nasty girls looking at your print."

"Who's looking, Averly? We've been in this house so much the days are running together. I can't help it I'm blessed woman."

"Uh-hum. Hurry up with that janky evidence."

I watched him go through a rotation of pictures he took from our wedding.

"When did you have time to take these?"

"I made time," he smiled. "I wanted to have some memories even if you were ditching me at the altar."

"If I did, why would you want memories of something so negative?"

"I don't know. To remind me never to fall in love again."

"Yeah, right. Probably already had that girl chihuahua in the cut waiting."

"That woman's name is Chastity and not at all. This black man doesn't cheat."

"He better not, or this black man gone be a eunuch," I kissed his meaty lips before going to take a shower.

Juanita said she was on her way to talk to me about something. Hopefully, it was good news about my father's case.

"Let me know when she gets here."

"Okay," Lexington didn't look up from his phone.

When I got to the top of the stairs, I could see Juanita pulling into the circle drive, so I went back downstairs. I didn't want to rush once I got into the shower.

"Look at you," Juanita ran up to me to rub my belly. Lexington just rolled his eyes.

I don't know what happened between them, but he's been closed off to her lately.

It could be the fact that she's an opp too.

"How have you been?" I asked her.

"I'm okay. Just stressed, still trying to round up everyone on this indictment. Some people have gone on the run. That is neither here nor there. I have a surprise for you," she handed me her phone.

"Hello?"

"Hey, baby girl," I could feel my dad's smile through the phone.

"I've missed you, daddy."

"I've missed you too, baby girl," his baritone voice was lighter than usual.

"Is everything okay? Are they treating you okay?"

"Yes, as well as can be. I'm working it out so that I can move around more until the trial, but they're scared the organization will get to me before the trial, so you know how that goes."

"Are you worried about them coming after you?"

"I can handle myself. How are you and the baby? Lexington keeping you both safe?"

"Yes, sir. We're going to renew our vows."

"Really? That's great. Don't flip out on that man again and leave him at the altar either, Averly Grace."

"I won't this time, daddy. I promise. You did well with your matchmaking, I guess."

"He seemed like a good kid growing up. Worst case scenario, I knew he would always protect you no matter what. If you both fell in love for real, it would be a best-case scenario. I'm not going to act like I didn't do it for my selfish reasons, but I did my best to try and make it work for the both of us."

"My life hasn't been normal. I don't know why I obsessed with a fairy tale love affair," I confessed to my father.

"I wish I would've had the courage to come clean with your mother about how I felt about Juanita. Maybe it wouldn't have gotten so messy."

"We all make our own choices. I'm not going to pretend to understand the choices either of you made. I'm just ready to move forward. I have a baby on the way. I have my own family now. The foundation is everything to me because of what I've been through."

"I can understand that. To show you that I'm doing my best to turn over a new leaf, Juanita will take you to your mother's grave."

My heart dropped into the pit of my stomach. A robin singing outside the window caught my attention briefly.

"Why now? I asked you for years. You would never tell me where she was buried. I thought you were lying about her being dead, to be honest."

"We never had her grave marked or got her a headstone."

"That was cold, dad," I hoped my dry tone choked him.

"I know. I'm trying to make things right. When Juanita takes you, let me know how much it cost to get a headstone and an area built so you can go and sit when you want."

"I'll pay for it. Where is the photo album so I can have a picture put on her headstone?"

"It's in my office on the bookshelf. They're all organized by year if the Feds haven't torn through the mansion."

"Okay, thanks for this, daddy."

"Anything for you, Averly Grace. I'm going to show you that I can be the father you deserve."

"You better, daddy. You have a granddaughter that's going to be looking up to you."

"A granddaughter? Really?"

"Yep."

"That's great! Papa Neri. That has a nice ring to it, don't you think?"

"Yes, I do. Take care of yourself, daddy. I hope to see you soon."

"You will, my love. I promise," he said, ended the call.

I felt a bit better after speaking with my dad. We had a long road ahead of us until we make it to this trial.

"Did he tell you?" Juanita asked.

"Tell her what?" Lexington's eyebrows wrinkled in confusion.

"Where my mother is buried," I answered my husband's question.

"Wooowww," he dragged out.

"I know, right. After all these years, I'm finally going to see where my mother is buried. I had started to wonder years ago if she was even dead."

"I can take you once you're ready," Juanita offered.

"I'm ready now. I've been waiting on this moment since I was a kid."

We piled into the car with Juanita. The agents assigned to us also jumped in separate vehicles to follow us.

"Juanita, do you think we can hire our own security detail?"

"Do you think you can trust anyone in the city?"

"I have some connections that I know will come through without hesitation. All have their license to conceal and cary. They are also professionally trained," Lexington assured her.

"They won't give you a problem about it. They're tired of footing the bill for the overtime anyway. They've been reporting that there's been no suspicious activity anyway. Let me know when they are ready to take over. I will end your protection with the agents."

"Why are they still allowing you to be around us? Isn't it some kind of conflict of interest?"

"They fought me on it tooth and nail, but I insisted on seeing this through."

"I bet you did," Lexington spat.

"Okay, what's going on?" My eyes traveled from Lexington to Juanita, waiting for an answer.

"Yeah, what's going on, Juanita."

"She doesn't need this drama right now, Lexington."

"What drama?"

"When I stepped into the hallway at the hospital, I overheard her telling that U.S. District Attorney that she wants to stay close to us just in case they need something from us during the trial."

"What? After everything you put us through, you still gone stand there and run my family through the mud some more? I can't believe you!"

"I had to tell her what she wanted to hear. Would you rather not have an inside man during all of this?"

"She makes a good point, baby. We do need to know what's going on and where they have my dad."

"You've known her longer than I have. Well, you thought you knew her. If you think she's on the up and up, then so be it."

"Juanita, if you betray my family again, I will kill you myself. I will personally watch you bleed out while I breastfeed my daughter."

"I won't! I'll prove it to you," she put the truck in park once we came to a stop in an open area in the cemetery. "Come so I can show you where your mother is buried."

She walked me to the center of the field. She was in a lot alone, it appeared.

"Why is she out here alone?" I asked Juanita.

"Your father bought the entire lot. He knew one day he would have to tell you where she was buried."

"There's no good reason he never told me other than spite. Even in death, he wanted my mother to suffer."

"They were complicated, but they loved each other."

"Until you came between them, right?"

"No, it was hard on your mother being in this family. It's why she clung so hard to Dasante. She thought she had someone who understood her."

"Can you just leave me here alone?" I asked them both.

"Sure," Juanita said.

"If you need me, I'll be right over here," Lexington kissed me on the forehead.

"Okay."

When they were out of hearing distance, I had an overdue conversation with my mother. You could smell the recently cut grass. I was just taking Juanita's word on this because other than a metal cross sticking in the ground, there was no indication this was my mom.

"All this time, I thought you were this helpless victim of dad's like I was all these years. Come to find out; you had a hand in creating this hell for me. I know it wasn't all on you mama, but really? Had you not been opening your pocketbook to Dasante, you would still be alive! I know how it can be being in love with two men, though. I'm pregnant and don't know who the father is. I'm praying it's Lexington's.

You would've liked him, mom. He's so respectful and attentive. When I'm with him, I know I'm safe. We have each other's back too!" I looked over at Lexington, whose eyes were fixed on me like a hawk.

"I'm really mad at you for leaving me to do life on my own without you. Every day, year after year, I miss you. Not a day goes by that I don't think about what life would be like with you here. What would've been prevented? I might as well forgive you along with daddy and Juanita. I'm trying to mature for my daughter. You know, chill out on the tantrums, although I think I'm too late. I know Alisha's going to give me a run for my money," I laughed, rubbing my itching belly.

"That's her name. Alisha, after the young lady who saved my life. That's another story on a different day. I'm going to stop by the office and order you a decent burial spot. I want to have one of those houses built for you. Instead of having them exhume your body, I'm going to build the mausoleum around you. It's going to be perfect. I love you, mama. I have to go now. We are staying low because daddy has turned on the organization. I know that would've made you smile. Your smile could dry up rain on the cloudiest day. Rest mama. I'll be back soon."

CHAPTER TWENTY

AVERLY GRACE

One week later...

"Averly, stop procrastinating and let's go," Lexington spewed orders like he was my daddy or something.

"I'm ready, geesh," I tossed my eyes around in my eye sockets. He's been getting on my last nerve. If this baby weren't his, it would still look like him the way he be pissing me off.

"Stop worrying. Everything will work out the way it should," Lexington tried to calm me.

"How can you be so sure?"

"Because I prayed about it. I know God has my back. I will love anything connected to you. Unless you hate them, then we can plot on how to kill them for sure," he nudged me.

"Already," I bumped my fist against his as we proceeded into our signature handshake we made up. It was cute and corny.

"Now, let's roll," he ushered me out the front door. Our security team was suited and booted like the Secret Service.

They were all lined up like they worked for Men in Black. It was dope and overwhelming all at once. We haven't received any backlash from the community, but we know it's coming.

We betrayed all of them. The one person they need to have in custody, they don't. Abra. They call him the White Glove. He wears them when he kills and cleans up his crime scenes. It's an art to him. He's the only one I've been worried about. I can handle the random shootouts. Abra was so skilled at what he did for my father that the Council made him the hitman for all families. They called him for the heavy hitters they needed to put down.

Lexington made sure our armory was fully stocked and functioning.

Despite how much I desired to bring my daughter into a different life, it seems I'm only putting her in the same violence-riddled life I lived.

I people watched as our driver maneuvered through traffic to get me back to the doctor's office, where I had my tests started.

It was bittersweet going back there. I dreaded being reminded of that imbecile Tonio and that backstabbing Grecia. Then again, I was about to see Alisha again. Had she not given me that phone and a head start to get away, who knows if my husband would've found me in time before they moved me again.

The same chick I felt was helping Tonio, and Grecia was sitting at the desk on her phone. I wanted to smack those green contacts out of her eyes.

"Name and date of birth?" She didn't bother looking up to give me a proper greeting.

"Averly Grace Charles and my-"

"Oh, I remember you," she twirled her pen while grinning at me. "You okay, girl?"

"I'm fine, but I'll be better once I'm done suing this office for a privacy violation. Mind your business and get me checked in Dreka," I squinted my eyes to read her name tag.

She sucked her teeth, but I didn't hear a peep out of her after that.

"Mrs. Charles?" The nurse who came out last time I was here gently smiled as she motioned with her clipboard for me to come back. "Now, is this one holding you, hostage," she slyly whispered so that Lexington couldn't hear her.

"No, this is my husband. He rescued me and hasn't left my side since."

"Well, that makes me feel better. Once I get your weight, I'll walk you down to the room at the end of the hall, near the exit," she winked.

I told her that I was safe, but I guess they weren't taking any chances.

I stood on the scale as she scribbled something in my chart. When I was done, I followed her into the room at the end of the hall.

"Stop twirling your hair with your nervous butt," Lexington gently grabbed my hand that was nursing a strand of my hair.

There was a tender knock on the door.

"Come in," I answered.

"Hello, Mrs. Charles," Dr. Statmoor had a smile as wide as Texas.

"Hello, Dr. Statmoor."

"Well, it's nice to meet you! I'm so pleased that you're okay. I heard about what happened."

"Yes, it was a traumatic experience, but the baby and I are okay. Aren't we?"

"We're going to check today. I also have your results from the DNA sample. We were able to get that much done while you were here last time."

"That's great."

"Well, go ahead and get changed into this gown," she patted the stacked garment with her hand. "One of the nurses will come to get you and take you to the ultrasound room. Do you already know the sex of the baby?"

"Yes, when I got shot, they gave me an ultrasound. I'm having a girl."

"Shot?"

"Yes, I didn't know your name, so they couldn't send you my records."

"Baby, you've been through it in such a short period of time. Which hospital did you go to? I'm going to request the records."

"Memorial Hermann Texas Medical Center," I told her.

"How have you been healing? Still extremely sore. They said it was a miracle that my daughter and I survived."

"I bet. Okay, get undressed. Let me get a hold of these records so I can see what else I need to look for."

"Okay. Thank you. I haven't been experiencing anything else. I feel like I'm back to my old self."

"Baby, it takes your body time to heal, especially from a gunshot wound. Let me just see what's going on. I'm glad you're okay, though."

"We are too," I looked up at my husband reading his thoughts.

We've come a long way in such a short period. I can't imagine life without him now. All the reasons I trusted him back in school proved to be true. I wasn't wrong about him.

Once the doctor was out of the room, I started changing.

"Let me help you, baby," Lexington offered once he noticed me struggling to get my blouse off.

He gently removed my shirt.

"Do I need to take your bra off too?" He gave a mischievous smile.

"No, I think I'm good."

"Because I don't mind," he insisted.

"I'm sure you don't," I giggled. I couldn't keep him off me these days.

His hands traced the wound that was healing from where I was shot, "I can't believe I almost lost you, Averly Grace."

"I would've just waited for you in the afterlife," I placed my hand over his.

"If you die, I die, woman. Ain't no living without you. I'm NOT living without you!"

"This dog on baby is making me soft," I complained, wiping the tears from my eyelids.

It's hard to believe that I fought being married to this amazing man.

There was a knock on the door again, "Come in."

"Hello, I'm Amanda. I'm your ultrasound tech. Are you ready?"

"Yes, I thought Dr. Stratmoor needed to look at my records from when I got shot?"

"She's still looking them over. She's given me some instructions on some areas she would like me to concentrate on. If there is anything else, she will have you come in for a follow-up."

"Okay," I got up from the small medical bed and followed her down the hall. "Is Alishia working today?"

"Yes, she's here today. Would you like to see her once I'm done?"

"Absolutely," I smiled so hard my cheeks hurt.

"Okay, I need you to get up on the table for me, please."

Lexington helped me up on the small stool so I could sit on the bed. It looked more like a chair with stirrups.

"Do you need me to raise my gown so you can put the KY on my stomach?"

"No, we have a different way of doing things now," she laughed, holding up what looked like a dildo with a string.

I watched as she put a condom on the wand. She squeezed some KY on it before approaching me.

"Okay, relax your thighs for me. I'm going to put this inside of you. This object is how we will do the ultrasound."

"Oh, shoot. I need to take one of those home with us, huh baby," Lexington nudged me.

"Stop showing out in front of this lady, please," I cut my eyes at him.

"As you wish," he chuckled.

"Do you want to hear the heartbeat?"

"Absolutely," I sat up slightly on my elbows.

She turned up the volume on the machine. I heard the most beautiful sound in the world, which was my daughter's heart beating-fighting for her right to exist in this world.

Lexington squeezed my hand a bit tighter as he stared at the screen, "I'm going to be a daddy Averly Grace," he cooed.

"Yes, you are."

Our love enamored the tech. She continued to click the mouse to complete the angles my doctor wanted.

"You did great. Your husband can help you down and back to your room. The doctor will be in shortly with your results from the blood test and to go over your sonogram results."

"Thank you."

As promised, when we made it back to the room, the doctor came in within about ten minutes.

"It looks like you are healing just as well on the inside as you are on the outside. Physically anyway. Are you seeing anyone for the mental trauma you've experienced?"

"Seeing someone?"

"Yes, like a mental health professional. I know in society, we normalize things that aren't normal. Getting shot is a big deal!"

"I know. I don't want to linger there. I have a life to live. I don't want to keep digging through something that happened that I survived."

"I understand, but please just think about it. Promise me you will."

"I will think about it," she squinted her eyes at me. "I promise."

"Okay. I'm holding you to it. When you come back for your follow-up visit, I'm going to ask you about this again. You don't have much further to go, so soon, we will see a lot of each other until you deliver."

"I'm ready to have my body back, so I welcome more time with you, Dr. Statmoor."

"I hear you," she chuckled. "I have the results of the blood test. Grecia is not the father of your child. It came back 99.9% that Lexington Charles is the father of your daughter. Congratulations to you both!"

"Thank you, Jesus!" I yelled. "You don't know the weight you just took off my heart," I sobbed.

"Don't cry, baby," Lexington pulled me close.

"Can we talk to Alishia?"

"Sure, I'll go get her. Once you're done talking to her, you can get dress and go home. I'll see you soon."

"Thank you again."

"It's my pleasure.

There was another knock on the door.

"Come in," Lexington and I both responded in unison.

"I heard a pregnant lady wanted to see me," Alishia joked, coming into my room.

I leaped from the bag and threw my arms around her like she was a best friend I'd lost touch with.

"I just wanted to thank you for helping me properly," I found myself yet again wiping tears from my eyes.

I nodded to my husband, who pulled out a thick letter-sized envelope filled with cash and handed it to her.

"What this?" She took the envelope and opened it.

"Oh my God," she gasped, dropping the envelope on the floor. "I can't accept this."

"You can, and you will. This phone is for you too," I pulled a brand new Galaxy S21 Ultra from my purse.

"Thanks, but I already have a phone," she laughed, trying to hand it back.

"Well, keep it just in case another kidnapping happens."

"Lord, I pray not but duly noted," she shoved it inside of the envelope.

"One more thing. Guess what we're naming our daughter?"

"Drop the deets, girl!"

"Alishia," my lips spread from ear to ear from me smiling so hard.

"Shut up and keep on talking! No way! Now, that really is too much, you guys," her eyes watered.

"Had it not been for you, my baby and I could've died at the hands of those fools. I still don't know what the end game was. I shudder to think about it, if I'm honest. Just know that I appreciate you. My card is inside the box if you ever need me for anything. Alishia, I do mean anything," I stressed.

"Thank you. I would do it all over again. I wish I would've done more. I'm just glad it worked out."

"We are, too," Lexington said.

"Well, I won't hold you," Alishia hugged me once more before leaving the room.

"You ready, Ms. Lady?" Lexington asked.

"Yes."

"I need to get you home. I got a wedding to top," he teased.

"Boy, please. I bet your joint doesn't look better than mine," I punched him in the chest. It was like hitting a brick wall; he was so muscular.

"You gone see," he smiled, escorting me out of the office.

I was low-key excited that he was planning our vow renewal. I have the best husband ever.

CHAPTER TWENTY-ONE

AVERLY GRACE

One month later...

"I can't believe I allowed Lexington to talk me into a vow renewal knowing I'm as big as a house," I fussed, trying to fit into my dress.

Sadness crept inside of me. I wished my mother was here to help me on my special day. It would be nice even to have Juanita here.

I pushed those hopes aside because the new norm was just me, my husband, and our security team.

I wish I could trust people growing up so that I could've formed some levels of friendships in my life. A best friend to hold my hand while I cried or vented about the little things that Lexington does to drive me crazy.

After struggling for nearly an hour, I was finally dressed.

We opted for a small ceremony in our backyard. I couldn't front; Lexington did his thing. The wedding tent covering was sheer with peach silk accent fabric weaved throughout. Fresh bleeding heart flowers rested in tall vases that were more than half my height. Candles were lit everywhere, giving it a soft ambiance.

A lady was off to the side playing the harp. It sounded like I was being welcomed into heaven. The sounds were so angelic and peaceful.

Security surrounded us and patrolled the property. We had turned on the family, so our vow renewal was more like an intimate date between my husband and me.

"Daddy?"

"Hey, baby girl," he wrapped his arms around me. "Pregnancy compliments you."

"What? How?"

"I was able to work something out," Juanita walked in with a gang of dudes in suits with her.

"I wasn't about to miss your special day. When I heard about it, I told them I don't care how dangerous it is. I'm going to my daughter's ceremony. I wasn't about to miss you walking down the aisle again."

My father didn't have the opportunity to give me away when Lexington and I ran off to the courthouse.

"Thank you, daddy," I leaped back into his arms like I was a kid again.

"We're getting ready to start," one of the guards came over and told us.

They were starting to feel like family they're with us so much. They rotate shifts, but it's the same team.

There were a couple of them that I didn't recognize, though. I made a mental note to ask my husband about them.

When I heard our song This is why I love you by Major, my heart stuttered.

I found love in you
And I've learned to love me too
Never have I felt that I could be all that you see
It's like our hearts have intertwined into the
perfect harmony

This is why I love you
Ooh this is why I love you
Because you love me
You love me
This is why I love you
Ooh this is why I love you
Because you love me
You love me

I locked my arm with my father's as we made our way down the aisle. At the end of the path was the best gift my father forced on me, Lexington Charles.

"You are breathtaking Averly Grace Charles," my husband's warm breath tickled my ear as he whispered in it.

"Thank you," I blushed.

His pastor was conducting the renewal. Lexington insisted he be the one to perform our vow renewal. He wanted him to pray over us and our marriage.

The exchange of our vows was quick. It took less than an hour. For that, I was thankful despite wearing flats. My feet were still swollen, and my back was killing me.

"I present again to you, Mr. and Mrs. Lexington Charles," the pastor grinned with pride.

TAK!

TAK!

TAK!

TAK!

TAK!

TAK!

Our security team and the Feds quickly returned fire coming from the caters and those two guards I didn't recognize.

"Get down!" Lexington threw himself over me while letting his Beretta rip.

The pastor dove behind the platform dodging the bullets that came his way.

"Lexington! The baby is coming!" I moaned in agony with my hands between my legs. My water broke, but I technically still have three weeks left until Alishia made her arrival.

I could care less about the flying bullets. The only thing I cared about was my daughter making it in this world safe.

More guards rushed over to shield me, Lexington, and my dad.

Through a small opening under Lexington's arm, I could see Juanita with a gun in each hand running down the assassins.

The Bloody Six had been too quiet. We knew retaliation was brewing, but we didn't know when it was coming.

How did they even get in? Lexington was meticulous about screening anyone coming onto the property.

Someone sent them off because there was no way they were walking out of here alive.

"Neri, cover her!" Lexington called out to him as he stood.

"Baby, where are you going?" I moaned through another contraction.

"To end this! I need to get you to the hospital!"

I watched my husband reload and sprint towards the action. It wasn't long after until everything got quiet.

"Are you okay, baby?" My father asked me.

"Yes, daddy. I'm in a lot of pain. This baby is coming now!"

"Just hang on a bit longer baby," he pulled out his phone and called 9-1-1."

"Daddy, you calling the ambulance? The Feds already here."

"Unless they got a bus, you still need some paramedics to get you to the hospital!"

Sweat drenched my father's button-up white shirt. He had removed his jacket already to put it under my head.

"Ahhhhh," I screamed.

It felt like my back was snapping in half. It was as if every contraction was knocking the wind out of me.

"Get this baby out of me! Daddy, it hurts!"

"Hurry up, please!" I heard him on the phone.

My dad wasn't accustomed to my raw emotions.

"Is this normal?" I looked down. My white dress was decorated with bright red blood, like the first day of my menses times three.

"I'm here," Juanita grabbed my hand.

"Where is Lexington?" I questioned her.

"He's coming. He's helping my team make sure everything is secure. They don't know the property that well. We want to make sure this wasn't a diversion for something else."

"We called the paramedics. Lexington told me your water broke."

"I called them too," my dad told her. "Are they all dead?"

"Yes," she answered with no elaboration. I could tell this irritated him. "I warned you this could happen, Neri. We need to get you out of here as soon as the paramedics arrive!"

"I'm not going nowhere until I make sure my daughter and granddaughter are okay!" He spat. His face was beet red. Juanita knew what that meant.

Once daddy started looking like a dirty radish, he wasn't budging on what he said.

"Fine, Neri," she huffed.

I could hear the rattling of the stretcher once they arrived.

"How far apart are the contractions?" One of them asked.

"About three minutes or so," my father nervously replied.

I've never witnessed him so unnerved. Years of me thinking I was nothing but a piece of property to him was not true. My father loved me and only did what he thought was best for me. He knew I would never abandon my loyalty to the family to marry Grecia. Despite Lexington being the son of Dasante Charles, he knew that he would love me and protect me with his life. My safety was something my father was plagued with. What would happen to me if he were to die? He trained me to take care of myself, but I was such a spoiled brat who was stuck in her ways.

The last several months has made me not only a woman but a wife and mother. I was proud of my growth.

They rushed me up to labor and delivery as soon as we pulled up. Lexington was hot on the wheels of the hospital bed.

"Mr. Charles, let's get this gown on you," One of the nurses handed him a disposable gown and cap.

They carefully got me out of my soiled dress and into a gown that opened in the front. They put these elastic bands around my waist that monitored my baby.

I breathed a sigh of relief, "Is she okay?"

"Yes, but we need to get her out of you as soon as possible. Your placenta has ruptured," Dr. Statmoor told me.

"I didn't think you were going to make it in time."

"Your husband called me and told me what happened. I hope after this baby, your life gets a bit more peaceful. For now, let's focus on getting baby Alishia out of you," she smiled.

"Ouuccchhh," I cried again. "How did you know what I was naming her?"

"Are you kidding me," she positioned herself between my legs. "Alishia been telling everyone in the office," she laughed.

"Okay, on this next contraction, I need you to push for me."

"Okay."

"You got this, baby! I'm buying you the best push gift ever, I promise," Lexington encouraged me.

I pushed but to no avail. Alishia was not budging.

"It's okay. Breathe and puuussshhh," Dr. Stratmoor coached her.

It was eight long hours before Alishia made her arrival.

"Why is she not crying? Why don't I hear anything, baby?" I panicked.

"I'm sure she will be okay, right, Dr. Statmoor?" Lexington's question sounded more like a threat than anything.

She didn't respond. I could feel Alishia between my legs still. Out but still on the bed.

"What's wrong with my baby?" I screamed.

Lexington's eyes were fixed between my legs.

She finally let out a scream that gave me relief. I plopped back on the bed in exhaustion.

"Is she okay?" I asked again.

"Yes, she's fine," Dr. Statmoor finally answered. "Birth is just as hard on babies. The pediatrician is checking her over while I get you together. You want a husband stitch?"

"Yes!" My husband answered for me.

"Wait, what is that?" I asked her.

"Alishia tore you just a bit. I need to stitch you up, but I can put a few extras in to make your opening to your vaginal area tighter. Basically, not like a virgin again but, they call it a husband stitch for a reason," she laughed.

I cut my eyes at Lexington, "I guess."

"Here is Alishia Charles," one of the nurses handing me a beautiful baby girl with a head full of cold black hair and pale skin. Her ears were chocolate like my husband's.

I smothered her with kisses. She was so content laying on my chest.

"Do you want to hold her baby?"

"She's so little, I don't want to hurt her," he replied nervously.

"You won't," I carefully laid her in his big arms.

I could look into my husband's eyes and see him fall in love with her instantly.

"She favors your mom," he smiled.

"I thought so too."

"Alright. We're going to get the baby to the nursery to get cleaned up and get bloodwork done. Mom, we're going to get you cleaned up as well so you can relax until we bring the baby in for a feeding. You are breastfeeding, right?"

"Absolutely."

"Okay, we'll bring her as soon as they let us know you're settled. Your family will be able to see her from the nursery window shortly."

"Okay. Lexington, can you let my dad know that I'm okay? When can my father come to my room?"

"If he can give us a few hours to get you settled, your husband can bring them up."

"Thank you."

*   *   *

THREE HOURS LATER. Once I was comfortable and in a clean gown, they brought my daughter in.

"She's a bit fussy because she had to get bloodwork, and she's hungry."

"Hey, muffin," I cooed. "Ready to eat?"

I attempted to put my nipple in her mouth, but she acted as if she didn't want it. After a few tries, she latched on.

"You're so beautiful," Lexington was staring strangely at me.

"Why are you looking at me that way?"

"Because you're breathtaking. Just to watch you nursing our daughter with no makeup. Your hair pulled up in that messy bun is so authentic. I would do anything to keep you both safe. You know that, don't you?"

"I know, baby. Is everything okay?"

"Yes, just with that trial and what happened today, I'm about ready to take you and her off the grid until it's time for court."

"That's an excellent idea. I don't even want to know where you are," my dad said, entering the room.

"Me either," Juanita agreed. "I'll figure out a way to communicate the date the trial starts."

"Well, it should be plastered all over the media. We should be able to find out that way. You have six of the largest crime families in the city on indictments under the RICO Act."

"That's true—all the more reason for you all to disappear. You don't have to testify, so there is no need for you to come," Juanita insisted.

"I have to be there for my dad," I debated.

"No, you don't," my father assured me. "I don't want to worry about you, the baby, and Lexington. You are all I have left. Once this is done, I just want to be a papa to my grandchild and spoil her rotten. I want to make up for everything I did and got wrong with Averly Grace," he sighed.

"You got it right more than you got it wrong, dad. It didn't seem like it, but I think I came out okay. A bit bratty but well rounded."

"Definitely bratty, but we've worked on that," Lexington teased.

"If anything changes, Juanita, we need a way for you to contact me."

"I promise I will figure something out. It's going to take them months to build this case."

"So I have to be without my dad until then."

"It's a small price to pay for his freedom."

"I guess you're right."

"Well, enough of that. Let me enjoy my granddaughter," my dad reached for Alisha, who was breastmilk wasted.

After I burped her, I handed her to my dad. This moment was bittersweet. I had my own little family to worry about now, and my dad was right. It was about keeping Alishia safe and not leaving her without a mother like I was.

"He's got this," Lexington whispered in my ear.

The creases in my eyebrows straightened as my worry lifted slightly. I reminded myself that Neri Saccone is a savage and has earned his stripes. He can take care of himself. Besides, Juanita has his back.

I leaned back and decided to stop fighting my heavy eyelids. My life had finally come together. Daddy will go into hiding with Juanita until the trial, and Lexington and I will go off the grid to raise our daughter in a safe environment. This time no guards. Just us and a full armory. Can't no one protect us like us if push came to shove. Until then, we would live in peace.

CHAPTER TWENTY-TWO

GEORGIA WOODS
United States District Attorney

"I don't understand why she's still being allowed to be on this case. She has a conflict of interest!"

I was doing my best to keep my cool with the Deputy Director, but I was about to lose it on him.

"Look, she is a Special Agent in Charge! She did what she had to do to bring down the most powerful families corrupting this city! She passed all screenings and a polygraph!"

"You train them to pass those things!"

"What is the problem? The closer she stays to Neri Saccone, the more information we can get to build your case."

"Yeah, but I want them all, including her. I think she's dirty!"

"Get out of my office those unfounded allegations. You're a U.S. District Attorney, not an investigator. Stay in your lane Georgia!"

"It's Mrs. Woods while I'm at work! Don't think because I'm screwing you that I'm not going to do my job."

"I know you will do just about anything to advance in your job," he mugged me.

Austin Easton was fine, driven, and unforgiving. I cheated on him while we were together. He dropped me without hesitation.

I cheated on him while we were dating, and he's convinced it was to seal my new position as U.S. District Attorney. I earned that spot from hard work, dedication, and the right connections! He can go to hell in gasoline drawers, for all I cared.

Trust I wasn't thirsty for no man.

"If you can't stop making this personal, I'll file a report on you," I threatened.

"No, you won't," he arrogantly replied.

He was right. We weren't together, but when he called, I gave in. Not because I was still in love with him, but we had amazing sex, and there were no strings.

"Don't say I didn't warn you," I spat, leaving out of his office slamming his door.

I took pride in handling myself with poise and class. I got out of character and hood behind closed doors, but I had it together in the public baby.

I was a black U.S.D.A. I had to be better than all the rest. If he wanted to stand behind her, then so be it.

I pulled out my vibrating phone. It was my potential informant that would be the nail in the coffin on this case.

"Hey, I was just about to call you. Did you decide if you're in, or do I have to put you behind bars with the rest of them?"

"I'm in," he said, hanging up the phone.

This case will change my life! I'm already waiting on my Good Morning America, and Oprah calls. Houston is finally ridding the city of the most vicious families we've had the displeasure of being plagued by. I placed my firearm in my purse and grabbed my briefcase. Tomorrow I get to work in burying the Bloody Six for good.

The End